THE

TERRORIST

A
SEAL
Gone Bad

by

John Carl Roat

ISBN:ISBN-10: 1530856728

ISBN-13: 978-1530856725

DENIAL

This book is a total load of bull ka ka. I made it all up in my fertile strange mind. I would hope it is an enjoyable read and that a few of my thoughts give you something to think about and a few Laughs.

Remember: "Life is a bowl of cherries. The only problem is, cherries have pits, and most people don't like the pits. Get use to them, no pits, no Cherry Trees, no Cherry Trees, no Cherries. That's how God made things work."

The above is a Roatism! They help me explain this strange life to myself.

DEADICATION

This book is dedicated as I am: To my best friend and bride of over 50 years Judith Jo

John Carl Roat

Chapters	

The Short Version!

If you are only interested in how to put an end to my current activities, not how I became the Terrorist, you don't need to read past this page! If you want to learn about me and why, THE TERRORIST, read past this page.

It boils down to a few simple facts: We are a Blessed Nation of people. Some choose to call it American Exceptional-ism; I call it; being blessed with our Constitution. We never have lived to it but when we get close to doing so we are at our best!

You want to put me out of the Terrorist business? Start to live to our Constitution again; when your moving in that direction I'll go away: **This is the End Game!**

The Preamble of: **THE CONSTITUTION OF THE UNITED STATES**

"We the People of the United States, in Order to form a more perfect Union, establish Justice, insure domestic Tranquility, provide for the common defense, promote the general Welfare, and secure the Blessings of Liberty to ourselves and our Posterity, do ordain and establish this Constitution for the United States of America."

Study it, Learn it, Live it!: *http://constitutionus.com/*

If you're reading this, it means at a minimum: I am no longer Karl Austin but still walking among you. The Government of the United States of America now knows some of the crimes I've committed and they have capitulated to Demand Number 1: Allow Publication of this book without abridging any of it, not one damn word.

What did they get: One year of me staying clear of any terrorist activities. (Just so you can start getting an idea of how firmly I have our governments ga-who-lees in my grasp: They had to agree to this without knowing the content of this book.)

The Young Terrorist

I'm not sure what my first memory is. Before my brother was born they are just jumbled. After three, the memories become a strange chain. Sometimes the links are taut and the chain runs true, sometimes the links are slack and the chain wanders every which way. The best thing for me; I rarely remember being bored.

I'm called a terrorist,nasty word, in all truth I spent ten years planning and becoming not a terrorist but THE TERRORIST. Yes I think I have a large ego as well, some things in this life require a big ego. You don't take on hundreds of millions of people, by yourself, without a big ego. I think everyone will agree: I'm at least the biggest pain in the ass the good old U. S .of A. has had in a very long time.

I'm not writing this to apologize, or even to get you to agree. Frankly I don't give a shit how you feel about what I'm doing. There are only three reasons to do the hard work of putting my strange thoughts down in words. First, after all the pain my actions have caused, you deserve at least to hear why, directly from the horse's mouth, or ass, you choose. Second, there's a lot of down time being THE TERRORIST and I hate boredom.

As you will see, from the links in this strange chain that I'm laying out for you, "the good, the bad and the ugly", I'm no victim turning on society. It's all my choice and

John Carl Roat

for the most part, I'm enjoying the hell out of it. Third our government has been covering up the truth about what I'm doing and how to put it to an end.

I was born Karl John Austin, before my first brother Jim was born, I have only one bad memory, the rest are warm and fuzzy, a lot of being held, loved, and the only word that seems to fit, safe. I was the first, child, grandchild and great-grandchild. It’s odd that the only bad memory of that time is one of the clearest of my life. I was potty trained, and very proud of my BIG boys' underpants, no diaper, and as long as I didn't mess my pants, there would never be another. My poor mother had been in a struggle with me since I found out how to take the damn thing off. It didn't matter where we were, what we were doing, if she turned her back the diaper came off.

My teenage Aunt would stay with us. She was the only one in the family who would not let me in our only bathroom while she was in it. You know how it is when a kid is outside having a good time playing: if they got to go, they wait till the last minute. Well believe me; I was full of crap that wanted out. I ran into the house straight to a locked bathroom door, and of course Aunt Jo wouldn't let me in. The memory of standing there getting madder and madder, trying to hold that crap back is very clear. Clearer yet is the shame of my Mother and Aunt taking off my pants to clean the mess I could not hold back.

The links in my chain start being connected sometime

a few months before one of the biggest events of my life, the birth of my first brother. When I understood some of what my Mother and Dad were trying to tell me, I became very excited. I knew it would be a sister, just what I wanted. My Aunt Dee was just one year older than me, and we got along great. She had long brown hair, big brown eyes, was supper smart and forgave me anything.

I wanted one just like her. In those days they couldn't tell you what the little human was going to be. You didn't find out till it appeared. I thought about having a sister, till just after the call from the hospital. A brother? . . . I knew what a sister would mean; it would be just like Aunt Dee. I had not thought about a brother. The next few days went slow. I wanted my Mother and I wanted her now.

Finally Dad brought Mother home, she hugged me, told me she loved me, and showed me my new brother. He was little; he smiled a lot, had on a bunch of clothes, wiggled all over and made strange noises. I guessed he was all right. Anyway I had my Mother back and It didn't take too long before I was into the big brother thing.

Jim was just a few months old and had one of those swings that hung from hooks in the doorway. I was allowed to swing him as long as I kept him straight and didn't push him too high. My big problem was Jim liked going high, the higher I would push him, the harder he would laugh, and I loved to hear him laugh. Mother and

THE TERRORIST

I had the diaper war all over again.

Every time she turned her back, I would push him higher than allowed and Jim would laugh. The higher I pushed him, the harder he laughed. Finally, Mom got tired of the war and dropped the big one on me: if I pushed him too high again she would give Jim back to the Doctor. I surrendered instantly; my thought was if she can give Jim back, she can give me back too. That threat is the first time I can remember thinking something out. I did not want to lose Jim; plus if he could go back, so could I. Still, I didn't believe she would do it, but Jim's laugh wasn't worth what I could lose.

My Dad would take me anywhere with him but WORK that magic place he went to earn our food. I knew what work was, he told me it was what we did to live. Mother and Dad both worked at home and I had work too, my main job was helping my mom.

A little leap forward here, there are no weak women in my family. When you're a little person, you learn quickly where the power is. There was no one around me without power, I was surrounded. You got love all the time. You got respect if you did the hard work of life.

I could not articulate this, until "Women Liberation" hit me in the face. I thought all families were like mine, dumb me. The worst trouble I ever had from my Dad was when I didn't give my Mother the respect she deserved. Deserve and respect, my folks worked hard to drive that standard into my stubborn, obstinate, bullheaded, headstrong, in-compliant, intractable brain. Dad told me I didn't get my Mom's chair or carry something for my Grandma because they were weak, I should do it because women go through things in life men never do. As hardheaded as I am, I could see he was right. I felt my brother grow in my Mother and that was never going to happen to me.

My first clear memory of Dad and me; is one of those disconnected links in the chain, pre-Jim. Dad was a pilot in the Army Air Corps so he took me flying. The plane had two wings, one over the other. I think I got sick, but what sticks in my mind is that my Dad took me with him to a dangerous place. As I look back, that is the first time someone paid me the high honor of going into danger with me.

As a toddler someone had given me a sailor suit. That suit affected my life more than anyone could imagine. From then on, I was always going to be a sailor. The Halloween after Jim was born, I wanted to wear my sailor suit. Mother said she didn't know where it was, and that it wouldn't fit me anymore. I looked everywhere. No sailor suit.

The costume I wore that year showed me what true hate is. Mom made her mind up that I was going to be a girl. There are no words to describe what I felt, HATE for her and everyone who said "What a pretty little girl." I didn't know why she made me wear a dress, I thought I had done something wrong. Poor Mom, I used that against her till I was long gone from home, whenever I was in the wrong I could think about that dress and get madder at her then she was at me.

When you're three years old, you think your twenty-year-old dad and nineteen year old mother, are old people and know everything. Thank God they were more forgiving than I; they might have given me a late term abortion, any one of a thousand times before I left home. You can thank those two very tough, loving and patient people for me.

Just before we left Michigan for Sunny California, my Aunt Betty was to get married. Mom was part of the wedding so we were staying with friends in the big city, Flint. Being four and a half I was allowed out in the yard by myself, Jim, being a little guy, had to stay in the house with the women. Mom said it was too cold for Jim.

The yard had a fence and a gate so the ladies thought they had me safely locked down. I walked in the house got my hat and gloves and told Mom I was going to Aunt Bettie's. Mom looked out the back, saw the gate was locked and said, “Have a good time.” I couldn’t climb over the fence or gate but I could climb a tree, get on the garage roof, and jump onto a big pile of sand in the driveway next door. Of course I had learned by that age: Don’t let your Mother know everything you can do!

I don't know how long it was before Mom started looking for me, but she and the police didn't catch up with me, till I got to Aunt Betty's. The whole trip was no more than four miles. But it lasted long enough for a young boy to drive his poor Mother to the very edge. The police were not happy; they even mentioned they could take me to jail.

My only real problem during the whole trip was crossing the main highway that ran through Flint. I had never crossed a road with so many cars speeding by and was smart (afraid) enough to stand there and wait. Soon a great big black lady came across the road. She just stuck out her arm and the cars stopped. I thought the drivers were afraid of her. Someone hollered something I didn't understand.

She just stopped in front of the car, put her hands on her hips, and gave him one of those looks, I knew from the women in my family. He shut up, just like I did when my Mom gave me THAT LOOK; it meant STOP NOW. She just turned around and walked the rest of the way across the road, the man kept his mouth shut and drove off.

The Lady walked into a small store. When she came out and started back across the road, I just followed her. She didn't know I was there till we got to the other side. She saw me when I stepped up on the sidewalk, and asked me where my Mother was. I looked up at that lady and lied. I pointed down the street and said, "She's at my Aunt Betty's. She pointed her big black finger at me and said for me to stay away from that road and get myself back to my Mother. Who said children don't lie? My little butt moved down the side street, just as fast as my short legs would carry me.

I walked and walked, my legs were getting tired. I came to a gas station with a man standing by his car, while another man put gas in it. The man by the car had a hat on, and looked like my Grandpa Carl. I told him I was tired, and asked if he would take me to my Aunt Betty's. Both men started asking questions. Yes my Mother knows where I'm at. Yes I know where I need to go. I'm four years old. My Dad is at work. The two men stood there, talking and looking at me. The one, that looked like Grandpa Carl, put me in the car, and said, "show me where your Aunt lives." I stood there on the seat and pointed the direction. I didn't know the street names.

When he pulled up in front of the house my Aunt Betty came running out, pulled me out of the car and started hugging me. My Uncle to be, Gene, was talking to the man who had given me the ride. Next Mom and the police showed up. My mother was hugging and kissing me one minute then: I didn't understand what was going on, but my mother set me down and gave me THAT LOOK! I knew things were about to get bad for me. She had her hands on my shoulders and was bent over and looking me dead in the eye. She then said something very strange: "Look What You Did to My Hair!" It took me many years to figure out what that meant.

The girl that lived across the field from us was two

years older than me. She had taught me a game that I played with her anytime she would. We found places where no one could see us, took off our clothes, touched, and kissed each other all over. In the last big event in my life before the California trip, we got caught. We were in the chicken coop playing our game. Her little brother put his face up to the window and then left. The next thing I know her mother is shaking me all over the place. My girl friend was sent in the house with her clothes. Her mother then made me get dressed. That woman dragged me down the road by my ear, all the way home.

I was sitting on the porch, the women were out in the yard, they talked and talked, my mother kept giving me THAT LOOK. She was indignant. She kept saying, "Wait till your father comes home." Mom had never said that to me. She always took care of things on her own. She took me to my room and told me not to leave till Dad came home. I wasn't sure why I was in so much trouble. When Dad got home, I could hear them talking down stairs. When he came up stairs, he sat me down and said "There is nothing wrong with what you did, but you have to wait till you grow up and get married." We went downstairs, Mother hugged me and I told her I wouldn't do it again. I think they knew I lied; I did.

My first act of terrorism took place the day before we left for California. We had our trailer and were at my grandparent's house. My mother was their oldest child, three girls. Whenever the man next door was around my mother watched him like a hawk. She told me he was a bad man and to never be alone with him.

I don't know how I knew; but I knew that man had hurt my Mother and I hated him. Where a five-year-old child comes up with a plan I don't know, but I found a big nail down by the railroad tracks, where my friends and I played. Somehow I knew what to do with it.

That night I wedged the nail, point to the tire, fat head to the driveway, under the back of his front right tire. I slept on the front porch. It was closed in, but you could hear the cars going by on the street -- my favorite place to sleep. I was up early waiting for that old fart to move his car. I knew that tire would just blow up. When he got in the car, I held my breath and peeked over the edge of the window ledge. Nothing happened. He just backed down the drive. No bang at all, off down the street he went. I was in the kitchen, eating my breakfast, when the old fart knocked on the back door. His car, had a flat, and he wanted to borrow a tire from my Grandpa. I had nailed his ass, It sure felt great.

California Bound

California, the big adventure. We had a twenty-six-foot trailer and a 1936 Ford with a brand-new Mercury V-8 engine. Jim and I thought the trailer was the best thing ever. I was a man before I figured out how tight a space that was, for my Mom and Dad and two rambunctious little boys.

What a trip! Mom and Dad had made up all kinds of games for us to play, we sang songs and peed in a bottle all the way across this beautiful country. Mom doesn't remember the trip with the same fond feelings. She was cooped up with me, a child who today might be called hyperactive, and another who would follow me anywhere.

Jim had reached the advanced age of two. He would try anything, rarely cried and was curious about everything. He was always stopping and looking at something I hadn't seen. I learned as much from Jim as he did from me. I would stop and see what he was checking out. He would get a look on his face, which can only be described as intent, and would become very still.

During one of our many stops along the road Jim was watching me try to catch a lizard. I grabbed it by the tail. The lizard kept running. And I had a wiggly tail in my hand. I dropped that damn thing, jumped back, and took off after the lizard. If anything, losing its tail, seemed to make it faster. The damn thing just out ran me.

Jim was squatted down, with the tail between his feet, watching it flipping and flopping. He had that intent look on his face, and was slowly moving his pointed finger toward the tail. Jim touched it, pulled his finger back, then reached down and picked it up. That got my attention. The pointed end was held between his forefinger and thumb, the fat end was hanging down and jerked back and forth. Jim lifted it up by his face and looked at the end that came off. When it stopped wiggling you could see four little bumps coming out of the end. Jim wanted to know why the tail came off. I wanted the lizard.

We had family in Wyoming at a place called Green River, where our Great Grandpa had come out to homestead and do some preaching. We were going to the ranch he had homesteaded. For a radio kid, an avid listener of Bobby Benson and The B Bar B Riders, this was what the trip was all about. There were men named Norris, Ira and Francis. We learned the difference between cattle and cows, cutting horses and working dogs. The ranch house was built from handmade Adobe blocks. It had thick walls and was cool inside even during the heat of the day. Down by the river there was a big old water wheel that was used to irrigate the fields.

One of the highlights of my first trip to Green River was the shooting. Norris Jr. was a year older than me, and we both had our own Red Rider BB Guns. Gun safety was driven home hard: if you loaded your gun at the wrong time, if you didn't carry it right, if you pointed it at someone, if you shot the wrong thing, if you didn't unload it when you were done -- all were things that could get your gun taken away. The rule was, treat all guns as loaded, all the time.

Norris and I could shoot our guns, down in the dry-wash, behind the house. Our two main targets were cans and lizards. The cans were legal, the lizards were not -- that is, unless we wanted to eat them. We got caught. No, we didn't want to eat the lizards. The guns were put up. We were not allowed to shoot for the last two days of our visit. I don't know how long it was before Norris got his gun back, but mine stayed up for months.

There is only one other memory that stands out from the trip. We were somewhere in the mountains, stopped by a stream. The water was cold, clear and didn't come up to my knees. Jim spotted some small fish, so we were chasing them and having a ball. Mom was sitting on the bank, laughing herself silly. She asked us if we remembered the dam we had seen. Jim had loved that damn, so when Mom said let's build one he got all excited.

Mom and Dad took off their shoes and started showing us how to build our own dam. Dad took big rocks and spaced them across the stream. Mom showed us how to place small rocks and sticks to fill the gaps. Jim and I went crazy, trying to stop the water. The higher it got on the upstream side, the faster it flowed over our rocks. We enjoyed ourselves so much, we were tired from laughing and ended up staying two days at our family version of Boulder Dam.

The rest of the trip was just Jim and me, having our adventure. Somehow everything seemed about us. We were never made to feel that we were in the way, if we were not the reason; we were always made to feel a big part of how and why something happened.

The only other thing that stands out about the trip was seeing the ocean for the first time. In those days there was no smog. It seemed you could see forever on a clear day. Dad stopped at a spot on the side of the Coast Mountains where we could see the ocean. It looked like the edge of everything. For once, I was as quiet as Jim. The ocean was where sailors went, I would be a sailor.

In the 40s and 50s, Southern California was a magic place to live. It seemed to be made for us. Our first trip to the beach, Mom told us we were going the night before. Neither Jim nor I got much sleep, we were up before the sun. Mom and I would share a love for that place, where the ocean meets the land; Mother the sun and the breeze off the sea, me those pounding waves, and the taste of the sea.

It's funny how small things loom so large in our lives. Dad walked Jim and me down to the edge of the ocean, we were hand in hand walking around with the water just coming over our feet, we sat down, got our butts wet, and splashed each other. We sat with water running back and forth, past our butts, and watched Dad walk out into the ocean. Jim got quiet as Dad walked through the waves. Mom and Dad played with us, and tried to make me in particular, understand the ocean could be a dangerous place. They knew Jim would follow me anywhere. If I would be safe, we both would.

Sometime later, I asked Dad if we could go out further in the water. We were told to hold hands, and we could go out until the water cane to our knees. Jim held my hand and we walked slowly out. Everything was fine while we were moving, but when we stopped I could feel the water moving the sand from around my feet. It felt like the ocean was trying to pull me down. FEAR, like I had never felt, grabbed me. I threw down my brother's hand and ran.

That day is a clear, a strong link in the chain of my life. FEAR and SHAME, two of the major things that shape us in this life. Jim was crying, Dad was holding him and Mom was calming me. No one said a word about me leaving my little brother, but my shame was worse than my fear, I would never run from fear again.

Mom had a job at a drug store, and made clothes for all of us. Dad was going to school during the day and working as a carpenter, building houses at night. Most weekends, Dad, Jim, and I would sell sunglasses and peanut brittle along the side of the road.

School. Never believe that schools used to be a place of truth and learning. They just told a different set of lies than today, and loved little robots. School is where I found out I'm not like the rest of you, it took me the next twenty or so years to figure out why. I know my school years caused my Mom and Dad a lot of pain. It's where I began my struggle with myself and the rest of you. God Bless us all, we need each other.

In many aspects I was just a normal kid, games, Scouts, church etc. I wasn't then and I'm still not smarter, bigger, faster or meaner, what makes me unique is when I get something focused in my mind and want it, there is no QUIT. I will suffer anything to achieve my ends and smile for the chance. Most of you just want security. I know there is no such thing, and love it. When I figured out, I only had to answer to myself, and one ALL POWERFUL GOD, the game was on. Remember those two words, ALL POWERFUL.

One thing school in the good old days had right? Politeness, I don't care how smart you were, rudeness was looked down on, and would get you smacked, till you got the point. Pain is one of GOD'S great teachers. If you won't suffer pain brought by your action, you won't do the action. GOD is the great teacher, it's us who learn slow.

Throughout my school years, there were always one or two teachers, who demanded the most, of our growing minds. Whatever the subject English, math, science, gym, they created interest. Even in those of us whose gifts were small. I think there are still those motivators of young minds out there, but somehow they are no longer the standard we set ourselves to live up to.

We had a good life, Mom and Dad were both busting butt. Yet somehow they were there for; Church, Scouts, ball, family trips, all the things they thought would teach us lessons of life. I knew about dying but it hadn't been close yet. All of a sudden the Grim Reaper was giving us the once over.

RHEUMATIC-FEVER, Jim had it, and might DIE. The rules the Doctor laid down were hard, mostly he had to stay in bed. Jim had a radio, books, and games In our room. He was either in his bed, or down stairs on the couch. We had our room on the third floor, so Dad would carry him up and down those old stairs. The only advantage I could see in being sick was no school, but Jim missed it.

I was scared, not so much about death, but the fact of not having my brother. Fear has always put me at my best, I think of fear as my personal best effort tool. I caused no trouble while Jim was sick, it was the only thing I could do.

The big break came for me when the Doctor told my Mom, I could take Jim for rides in his wagon. I was pretty damn sure he wasn't going die. Mom would bundle Jim up and off we would go, just as far and long as we were allowed, we did not want to lose this privilege. When Jim was out, his Red Wagon was the center of all kid activity in the neighborhood.

Jim and I had a black Cocker Spaniel called Inky. He was a BAD dog, he would suffer any consequence to do what he wanted. Inky owed his happy home to the fact that Mom and Dad loved us, and we loved that dog beyond reason. His crimes included: tearing clothes from the close-line, jumping through closed windows, going where he wanted when he wanted and killing cats.

That dog paid attention to no one, but like me, while Jim was sick, he was on his best behavior. Inky would walk along beside Jim in the wagon, when we stopped, he would sit, even a cat could not move him from the side of the wagon.

Just before Jim was well enough to go back to school, a friend of my Mom's wanted to give us two little kittens. Mom told the lady she was sorry, she would like to have them, but our dog would kill them. The lady told Mom that dogs do not kill kittens.

Then she asked Mom, if Inky accepted the kittens would we take them. Our Mom thought a minute, knew she would have to save the kittens from "THAT DAMN DOG" and said yes. Why mom counted on Inky is beyond me, he had never done anything she wanted up to then.

The lady got two tiny little kittens from her car. She said their eyes had just opened. We all went to the back porch, where Inky had his box. I knew what would happen: Inky would take any pain a cat would give him, and not quit till the cat either got away, or was dead. Jim and I figured if the ladies weren't careful those kittens were goners.

Inky was laying in his box, he never even raised his head, no growl, he didn't move. The lady held the kittens down close to Ink's box. He just lay with his head on his paws and ignored us. Mom was standing there looking worried, the lady set the two little furry things on the floor and stepped back.

The kittens made mewing sounds, our cat killer did not move. Mom looked confused, In a soft voice she said, "I'll be damned!" Inky stood up, stepped out of his box, bent his head sniffed the kittens, and walked off the porch. Needless to say, we had two kittens. Mom got assurance from the lady that both kittens were male and the fun began.

Jim and I named the kittens Frick and Frack, we would laugh our selves silly watching the kittens crawling all over our dog. They moved into his box and even tried to nurse on him. Inky never paid any attention to them. They followed him anywhere they could. He didn't seem to know they were there. That is, until they had grown and started helping Inky run down cats.

THE TERRORIST

The first time Jim told me what he had seen, I almost didn't believe him. Our bad assed dog's only weakness in his on going battle with cats, was his inability to climb trees. Jim said he had seen Inky tree the big black cat from down the street. Nothing unusual there -- that cat would climb a tree the second Inky came into view. Jim said; Frick and Frack went up the tree and knocked the black cat off the limb and the chase was on.

Both Inky and I had been on our best behavior while Jim was sick. When he was better, we went back to our old ways. I discovered the spot on the trolley-car tracks that set off the crossing signal and brought down the gates. What a great tool in the hands of trouble making young boys.

The trolley ran from Long Beach to Los Angles and was a main target of several of the older boys and myself for committing minor antisocial crimes on. We would hide in the bushes along the tracks and throw rocks at the trolley. Sometimes we would place things on the tracks just to see what would happen when the trolley hit them. The object had to be small enough so the driver wouldn't see it to soon and stop.

One of the guys had put a penny on the track and it was flattened. I wanted one like it. When I was putting my penny on the track, I noticed a gap between two sections of track. I put one edge of the penny on each side of the gap, just then the crossing signal sounded two blocks down the track, we ran for the bushes.

We crouched there waiting for the trolley, No trolley:The signal was clanging and the crossing gate was down on Compton Boulevard, cars were stopped and no trolley. We waited a long time before the trolley finally came by. To top it off, I couldn't find my penny. There was some talk, that it may have stuck to the trolley wheel.

In those days a penny was big money, to a ten-year-old, I let two trolleys go by before I made up my mind to put my last penny on the track. When I placed it on the same gap and the crossing signal started clanging away, I knew! Pick up the penny, the signal stops. Set the penny across the gap, the signal starts. I picked the penny up and put it back in my pocket. I didn't want the other guys to know what was happening. I had to think about this: I could stop traffic!

After dinner Jim and I went across the park to the bushes by the tracks. I had told Jim that I could make the signal go off and the gates come down to stop traffic on Compton Blvd., but I wouldn't tell him how. We sat in the bushes till the first trolley passed. As soon as the gate on Compton was up, I ran out on the tracks and placed my penny. Clang! went the signal, down came the gate. We watched from the bushes for a few minutes, then we walked down to the crossing.

The trolleys were called, The P& E (PACIFIC and ELECTRIC) and there were two set of tracks, west bound, and east bound. The trolleys going west came through on the hour and on the half, east bound ran at quarter past and quarter to. We watched the traffic jam I had caused and figured out it could last for 30 minutes, if someone didn't remove my penny.

The police station was about a block away from the crossing, toward our house. We could see two policemen heading our way, Jim and I beat feet the long way around. I now had the tools for my first mass crime against You, society, I just had to think it out. At the time there was no purpose, I just didn't like us -- the group, society. As individuals we seemed a lot better. Somehow inconveniencing the mass was all right, and I was more then eager to see the group squirm.

After a week of scouting out the tracks, the traffic, the streets and alleys, between the two crossings, I was ready. Jim was in on the planning and preparation, but not the execution. We had measured the gap in the tracks and had enough pennies wired together to fill the space. Jim had a small hammer that was just right for pounding them home they had to fill the gap tightly or the trolley would knock them out, I wanted the gates down as long as possible.

I picked Monday, at 7:45, a quick little two block detour on my way to school. I was going to hit the Compton Blvd. crossing and the next crossing to the east. Pound two sets of pennies in for each crossing, one for the east tracks and one for the west. Then peddle my ass off to school. Somehow even at that young age I new the keys to success where good planing and execution. Keep It simple, with a quick in and out.

Ten minutes after placing the last set of pennies, I was at school. My escape route was planed so I would ride my bike past the two crossings that were shut down.

It was my only mistake. Two days later there was a damn good description of me in the local paper. Someone had seen me "Fooling around down the tracks", then got a better look at me as I rode by the crossing. That taught me: don't hang around and give people a good look at you.

It had taken them an hour to figure out what the problem was and another hour to clear the traffic. People in the 50s, just as now, used a lot of technology that they had no understanding of. Not the first idea of how it worked, just use it. The paper said it was Compton's worse traffic jam ever. I was very proud of myself, but knew it was just for Jim and me to enjoy.

Until my teen years I would share most everything with Jim, even my crimes against humanity. My brother never told. To me everyone seemed like liars and I enjoyed causing them as much of a certain kind of aggravation as my strange little mind could think up.

Even then, I knew you and I were different. It didn't bother me much. I didn't like you, and I did me. I apologize, not for what I have done, but for not liking you. Once I understood you work best under stress, I started to like you. Stress would be my job.

I had always wanted to be a Sailor, well around the

time of the big traffic jam, I saw a movie called the FROGMEN, staring Richard Widmark. I was to find my life's ambition and get in big trouble for that movie.

Dad had dropped Jim and me off at the Movie, told us what time he would pick us up and left. It was a weekend and there were a lot of kids at the movie, the line ran down the block and around the corner. Jim and I had been standing in line waiting for it to move, when this man came around the corner counting kids. He got to me and said, "You're the last one in." Since Jim was behind me, in line, this was a problem. How I handled that problem has affected the rest of my life and given me the tools to cause you great pain.

No one would give up their spot for our popcorn money, so I had to make a deal with Jim. I would give him my allowance for two weeks, 50 cents a week and all our popcorn money for a month. Jim would wait in the Drug Store Soda Fountain on the corner while I saw the movie. I new Jim would never tell, so all I had to do was get out of the movie a little early, BEFORE DAD came to pick us up. If I had done what was right I wouldn't have seen the movie, what then?

Now, in the old days there was just one screen at the movies. They would show previews, a news reel, a cartoon and two feature movies. The Frogmen had top billing so it was last movie shown. My plan to leave early was domed. At the end of the movie I was standing by the curtain at the top of the isle. I could not take my eyes off the screen. This was all I wanted --

lockout of a submarine, kill the bad guys, and blow things up. The words, The END, hit the screen and I ran like hell, knowing I had waited too long.

Dad was sitting at the soda fountain with Jim. They were both eating ice cream. Dad gave me THE VOICE, "Karl go to the car and wait!" By that stage of my life, when Dad used THE Voice, I knew how much trouble was coming, by the tone, not the words. The Voice wasn't loud -- it was strong. This time THE VOICE told me I would get it all. First the why, second, 10 hard swats, third, loss of allowance and fourth, no extras for two weeks.

As I stood by our car, waiting for Dad and Jim, the movie was playing in my head. I was going to be a Navy Frogman. I could take what I had coming. Most of you want to believe life should be without pain. God didn't make it that way, that's why you're so easy to push. That's why you need to be pushed. Just think of me as one of God's pain pushers.

The next couple years sailed along. We got Steve and from the day of his birth, he fit. To my young mind, no one in our family was much alike. We were all pieces of a puzzle that made one picture together and another apart. Steve, to this day, is the only person I'm sure was born a fully formed personality -- happy, easy to get along with, curious and a sight to behold when finally pushed to his BERSERK state.

Then Came Twelve

The world changed for my family and me when I reached the ripe old age of twelve. Looking back, I'm thankful they mustered enough love not to put me out of my misery. The next five years were miserable for me and I made everyone suffer. Jim must have thought someone had inhabited his brother's body -- no more mister nice guy. Life would never be the same.

Two circumstances, one inevitable, the other perception, brought the radical changes in me that damn near destroyed our family life. 1. Raging hormones. 2 The size of the human lie. My Dad, God Bless Him, wanted to raise good kids that could THINK. For Dad this meant, "evaluate the problem and take the necessary steps to over come it." He was an aeronautical engineer. Thinking was the most important tool you could possess. It led to everything else. At this stage of my life I would only think when Dad wasn't around or I wanted something real bad.

We lived in El Segundo California. In the fifties a magic place, just across the sand dunes the ocean but more important, the home of Ural Sarri, the best water polo and swimming coach in the nation. Our first day in town I had found the El Segundo Swimming Pool, commonly known as 'the plunge'. It was a huge building, housing a 25 by 20 yard pool with a separate wading pool for the little ones. As I came through the doors the smell of water and chlorine enveloped me. Sound vibrated my body. Through the windows that separated the lobby from the pool could see some kind of game being played with a ball. WATER POLO. I wanted to play and the man that could make that possible was Coach Sarri.

His rules to play were: belong to the Swim Team, maintain a C average while failing no classes, make all practices including swim a mile before school, every mourning. His rules, and he enforced them. It didn't matter who you were. The best or just adequate -- don't follow the rules you didn't play. He had taken the El Segundo High Team to the Olympics in 1952 and they placed fourth. Teenagers were unheard of in the Olympics during the 5O's.

In many ways he was like my Dad -- true to his word (rare even in those days), big, strong, hard as a rock, demanding and patient. I wouldn't listen to Dad, so wanting to play Water Polo, kept me just within bounds. I think my Mother and Dad were thankful for any help they got in bending me to fit within the limitations of human society.

Junior High and High School were times of inner turmoil for me. I could clearly see the world was built on lies, but I wasn't a very effective liar. I learned fast that you don't have to lie to liars. You could just say nothing and they would make up better stories then you could ever think of.

Case in point, after 6th grade I couldn't get little girls to play the games with me that I had been taught by the girl across the field. From five years old till junior high school, there had always been two or three girls that liked to play the game. All of a sudden I was trying harder then ever and getting nowhere. So when the guys were standing around telling each other what they had done to this girl, or that, I just kept my mouth shut and gave a little smile. Throughout school I had the rep. of a real stud. I never said I was, but then I never said I wasn't --a lie of omission. In some ways I am an illustrious liar.

Sneaking out at night, moving through the streets, most times by myself, just checking things out. I liked to take two hubcaps off one car, and put them on a car a couple blocks away. Take the two off that car and move on. Always ending back at the first car, that way everyone had four hubcaps, they just didn't match. It gave me great pleasure every time I saw my handy work driving around town.

I held several different jobs while still in school. Busboy, at Pat Mars drive-in Restaurant, box-boy at the Mayfair Market, part time life guard, clean up at Farmer John's slaughter house. Best of all, two summers, busting my young butt on Uncles Ira's cattle ranch. I had been raised to work hard. All work was respected in my family. There was no task that anyone was to good for.

Jim and my main jobs at home were the weeds and dishes. We had a huge back yard with a lot of fruit trees growing in very fertile soil --soil that grew an endless crop of weeds. It seemed to me they grew just as fast as we pulled the damn things. I swore if I ever had a home, no weed would ever be pulled. The dishes were a simple arrangement, take turns washing and drying. I was capable of confusing this simple sequence of labor, turning it into a major hassle just to figure out who did what last.

You would have thought Jim, being much smaller, would give his larger, and slightly nuts brother his way? Not Jim, he never wimped out. If I could take it, I could have it, but he never just got out of my way. Sorry brother.

In my sophomore year I made the Varsity Water Polo Team, KING SHIT. Our main rival was Whittier; they had come to El Segundo for our first game of the year. Many of us knew each other from AAU competition and surfing. Most of the Varsity and B Teams were sitting on the front steps of the plunge. I'm just sitting there, trying to be cool, when --GOD NO! -- here comes my little brother hollering, “Karl, Karl watch this.”

Jim is carrying a pair of crutches, and has his little asshole friend Pauli with him. If I try to ignore them, Jim will just keep at it till he has my attention. If I tell him to fuck off, he will flip me the finger, then I'll have to thump him, and for some damn reason I didn't like thumping him. Not that thumping would get rid of him anyway. So I watch, hoping the older guys pay no attention.

Jim whispered something in Pauli's ear and hands him

the crutches. Pauli walks down the side walk a little way, and Jim hides behind one of the big trees in front of the plunge. Pauli starts back our way, on the crutches, when he gets just past the tree Jim is hiding behind. Bam: Jim jumps out from behind the tree, and kicks the crutches out from under Pauli. Knocks him to the ground, beats the living shit out of him, takes his wallet, and runs.

Well he had everyone's attention now. Most of the guys hadn't been paying attention when Jim and Pauli walked up. Many guys thought they had just seen a mugging, and didn't know what to do when Pauli got up, and Jim came walking back.

Pure pride in my brother overcame even my ME, ME, ME, teenage brain. As Jim and Pauli were telling me what happened when they did it in front of Jerry's Market, everyone gathered around and listened. Kay Miller, the Baddest Ass senior anywhere, told Jim "Cool Kid, do it again." Jim did it again, this time everyone busted up. Jim had that big smile on his skinny self. It felt good to be his brother. He said he would see me later, they were going down town, to do their Trick. I forget who won the game that day but I will always remember what Jim did in front of the Plunge and what happened when I got home.

My little brother had managed to get himself arrested. It seems that they had done their trick at several locations around town, and gathered several little friends as they went. Jim had refined their little act a little as well. One of his buddies had a cast on his leg, so he had become the victim, an added touch of realism. What had blown Jim's socks off, was no one had done anything, all those grown ups just stood there, with their mouths hanging open, while Jim beat and robbed a disabled person. I know Jim was not happy when he did find that one person who would do something!

The last mugging took place on Main Street in front of the bank, across the street from the police station. The crime went down as usual, except for one very old lady who started beating the shit out of Jim with her purse. My poor brother was now rolling around on the ground being assaulted himself.

Needless to say the cops showed up, all of Jim's little buddies had beat feet when the old lady started her attack. The only two criminals apprehended where, the kid with the cast and James Paul Austin. That's what Mother called Jim when she was mad.

Steve and I didn't find out what happened till we were together in our room, that night. Steve just sat there in awe, while Jim told us the story. To this day I laugh when I think of that old lady beating the shit out of my little brother with her purse. I think mothers suffer more than is fair. They grow us inside their bodies, being stretched this way and that. Their chemistry goes all crazy, and then most of us spend our youth making life as tough for them as we can get away with. Sorry Mom, I love you.

My Mother was a pretty, no nonsense woman, who could do anything, but there was one thing about Mom I thought was damn strange. When things would go bad , you know the whole world turns to shit: Mom would do whatever she had to do, no tears, no sweat, just plug along till we were out of the shit. It didn't seem to matter how long it took, two days or a year, she didn't falter. Then two or three days past the trouble, Mom would just come unglued, shaking, tears the whole unsightly emotional mess. Hey everything was over, what is the problem?

For years I didn't understand, not till after my first fire fight at night. Then I understood. There is nothing more intense then a bunch of people trying to kill each other at night! I'm not talking murder, that's easy, I'm talking a bunch of well-armed and trained people trying to kill each other in the dark. I was proud that when things got tight, I had just done what I needed to do. You train for that kind of shit, but you never know, till you've done it. Later I laid in my bunk and, the only word that fits is, trembled. I don't know if Mom taught me to stay cool at bad times or gave it to me in her genes: Thank You Mom shaking like a leaf is no problem after the shit is done.

Neither Mom nor Dad drank much -- a beer or two on a hot day, some wine for a special occasion. Booze, I loved booze, beer, wine and tequila. From the start I never drank sensibly. Drink as much as you can, as fast as you can, get as drunk as you can. Old demon booze would become the hardest battle of my life.

THE TERRORIST

My first run-in with the law over drinking happened one Saturday night. We had gotten one of the town drunks to buy us a case of T-BIRD wine. There were five of us macho young idiots, trying to out-asshole each other. I won by chasing a bunch of kids, who were minding their own business, off the basketball courts down at the recreational park.

I was so stupid drunk, that instead of hauling ass out of the park when the cops showed up, I ran around the park, like we were playing tag. Well, I was IT. The cops in EL Segundo were a good group of guys. They would just pour out your booze, and follow you home. That is, if you hadn't been causing trouble. I had, so they took me down to the station and called my Dad.

Now a drunk doesn't have the sense to know fear so when my Dad showed up and was being easy on me, I thought all was well, no problem. He drove us to Pat MAR's drive-in, Dad ordered me coffee, and let me order anything I wanted to eat. I had a big Cheese Burger, Fries and a Butter Scotch Milk Shake. Dad was sure being cool. When I finished eating, I lay down on the seat and went to sleep.

Dad shook me awake, and helped me out of the car. As I looked out of the garage my mother was standing on the back porch. She had Dad's robe on and rollers in her hair, her arms were crossed and she looked MEAN. I tried to get back in the car, but Dad wouldn't let me.

Mom met me in the drive, took me by my ear and

pulled me staggering along up the steps, through the kitchen, down the hall and into our bathroom. Mom was using extremely nasty words, this only happened when she was on the edge of VIOLENCE. Believe me ear pulling was not violence, it was for focusing attention. Pay close attention, or VIOLENCE happened. Even my drunk brain focused.

She pulled my ear down, and sat me on the edge of our half full bathtub. Mom's rollers were bouncing all over her head, she was screaming " Drink this you little shit!" She jerked my head around in front of a big glass of pink stuff. My head was jerked back, and Mom started pouring the pink stuff down my throat. It turned out to be Pepto-Bismol and salt.

As she poured the last of that foul crap down my throat, Mom pulled my ear back, and I fell in the bathtub. When my body hit the cold water, I started spewing large volumes of pink Cheese Burger, Fries, and butterscotch milk shake all over myself and my California Inter Scholastic Federation Championship Jacket. My only other clear memory as I puked and thrashed around in the ice cube filled tub, trying to get my jacket off, was FLASH, FLASH, FLASH. Dear old Dad had contributed the food and the photo memories.

You would think the little party, my Mom and Dad gave me, coupled with being grounded and loss of all privileges for two weeks, would end my drinking career. No, in some ways I'm the dumbest among us. I suffered much worse consequences, given with less love, for many years before I quit. I was well on my way to becoming an old wine-o with long nose hairs.

I have never needed more then four hours of sleep a night and can function well for thirty-six without any sleep, so even a school night was fair game to sneak out and do crime. I had to be in my bed no later then 5:45, so Dad could get me up at 6:00. I had my mile to swim, and he was always was at work early. We were both early birds, so on all our camping trips, Boy Scouts, church and family we would get up quietly, fix the fire and make breakfast.

We did some serious back packing and river trips. One that sticks out in my mind we saw and heard an atom bomb go off. We back packed up the John Muir Trail to a large plateau, just below the summit of Mt. Whitney. The campsite was a big disappointment; it was off the main trail at 11,000 plus feet and damn hard to get too.

No lake, no streams, we had to carry wood and water in from the 7,000 foot level, on top of our already heavy back packs. The men had not told us anything but that they would have a surprise for us after camp was set up and dinner done. We were not happy campers, bitch, bitch, bitch that's all you heard. No fishing, no wood, no water and no pine needles to make a soft bed.

All atom bomb tests in the 5O's were secret, so how the men knew, I don't know. That evening, around the embers of our cook fire, they told us what they hoped we would see and hear. We were the children of the

BOMB. I don't believe we feared it, more like we held it in awe. I know that bunch of teenage boys went from ticked off, to excited, quick.

Dad woke me at 2:30, we started a small fire and made hot cocoa and coffee. There was none of the usual bitching or dragging ass. When I held reveille, the guys were out of their sleeping bags and drinking hot cocoa in a shot. We all took flash lights, no moon just millions of stars in black night, and trooped off to the east end of the plateau. From that end of the plateau you look down over the lowest spot in the nation, Death Valley and east across the desert toward Nevada.

We sat looking east, singing songs. Right in the middle of "I've Been Working on The Railroad" a bright light, brighter then any star, appeared in the east and quickly expanded in a growing arch. There was enough light, when it had expanded to its fullest, to illuminate the desert floor.

It was dead quiet, we had stopped singing as the light expanded. Next came the sound, not loud but solid and deep, it went right through everyone and everything. The wave of sound made the mountains shake, for the next half hour you could hear rock slides crashing down the sides of mountains.

I truly love a good explosion and have blown up many things in my life but no explosion has ever impressed me near as much as that early morning atom blast, more then ninety miles away. Dad and the other men had given us something to think about for years to come.

Two Good Kills

The summer between 10th and 11th grade I was a box boy at the Mayfair Market over in Inglewood and found out how easy it is to kill people. Killing had not been my intent, I just wanted to hurt the son of bitches real bad. As it turned out they died too damn quick , and I learned killing the right person is no big thing.

One of the guys I surfed with from Westchester, told me about the job, he had been working there for a while and said, "The money's OK and you can swipe all the beer you want." Sounded good to me.

I had been saving money to buy a car since 7th grade. Dad said if I wanted a car I had to pay for it myself, he and Mom would pay the insurance and the car would be in their name till I turned 18. During the 5O's insurance for a kid didn't cost you an arm and a leg.

I got a hair cut and saw the assistant manager. The only questions he asked me, "What days and hours will you work? Any days and hours you give me." The job was mine.

In those days a box boy could make extra money by carrying out ladies' groceries and putting them in their car. That is, if you bagged or boxed them without squashing the bread, or bruising the fruit.

I only boxed when the store was busy, I was the new guy, so the crap jobs were mine. One of the jobs I liked, that no one else did, was stocking the shelves. I enjoyed making the shelves right, and if you stocked well, you got some early and late hours.

There was one guy that gave me a hard time -- the head box boy, lazy and always on some power trip. He was starting college that year, and had been with the market for three years. I couldn't figure how such a lazy, shit stirrer kept a job.

Twice a day I took the trash out and cleaned up around the dumpster. One afternoon that first week, I was cleaning up behind the dumpster. I heard some moaning, and the words “suck on it” came out of a small window just over my head. The voice sounded like the manager. I had to take a peak and see what was going on.

The window was glazed, but part way open at the top. I slowly crawled up on the dumpster, thinking I'm going to see the manager and some women going at it. The room was small, just a big closet with things on small shelves and kind of dark. I could see the manager’s back, his pants were down and someone was kneeling in front him. I was trying to figure out what was going on, when the manager moaned and slumped against the shelves.

WHAT THE FUCK! It was the lead box boy, he was sucking off the manager. I got down and got out of there. That was one ugly sight, now I knew how he kept his job.

One day the next week, we both got off at 9:00 pm. As I was crossing the parking lot to go to the bus stop, the lead box boy called me a cock sucker. He was older and bigger but I figured I could make him hurt. I dropped my stuff and ran at him hard. His first swing just missed my head, and down we went.

I wish I could tell you that I whipped his ass. I didn't. I had two black eyes, a split lip and my clothes were torn, but I just kept coming after him. His shirt was torn and he had a bloody nose, he quit. My baby brother Steve, let alone Jim, would never have quit with a piss-ant little bloody nose. I told him "Just leave me alone," and from then on, he did.

I had one good crime going on while I worked at Mayfair. I would walk around and load up a cart with groceries, just like when I was filling an order. I would put a case of beer under the cart and roll it to the parking lot. Leroy, Ron and Tank would be waiting in Leroy's 49 Ford, to pick up the stolen goods.

I never did this when the assistant manager was around. When it was just the manager, you could be sure he and the lead box boy would spend a lot of time in the manager's office closet.

A month passed with no problem. I made some tips boxing, a little extra selling the food and beer we had stolen, and enjoyed my job and the summer. One afternoon I put two cases of beer in the trash cart and dumped them in the dumpster. We would come back and get them later that night. I was standing there having a smoke when I heard a door shut and a little boy's voice saying "I don't want to do it, don't make me do it again." Then some soft crying. Next the lead box boy's voice saying "shut up!" and a loud slap.

I started being sick, and I ran, more afraid then ever in my life. I had no idea what to do, I couldn't even think. How I got through the rest of that day is beyond me. When I got home, Leroy came by. I told him where the beer was, but I couldn't go with them -- I'd see them at the beach in the morning. Thank God the next day was my day off I didn't think I could ever go back.

My mind felt like a pinball machine, everything was firing at once, bouncing all over my head. I told Mom I didn't feel good and went to bed before dinner. Anything that went down would have come right back up.

I lay in my bed for hours with my mind racing. I couldn't tell you one thought I'd had that night but when the racing stopped, I knew just what to do. The only reason I didn't get caught was dumb luck. The only plan I had was how to get them. Truly I didn't give a shit if I got caught: I just wanted to FUCK them both up!

The year before I had made a few bombs from gunpowder, gas, fertilizer, magnesium shavings and the such. Some had worked with varying degrees of success but one thing that I had done was simple but worked great. I took a cherry bomb and put glue all over it and rolled it around in Bee Bees. I let that set up and did it twice more. It was set off in an old shack at the end of the airport. It tore the place up.

I took two cheery bombs taped them together, twisted the fuses into one, and glued four coats of Bee Bees to my bomb. After I had my little surprise ready, the first time the assistant manager was not there, I struck.

It was so easy. I went out to get carts, walked behind the building --thank God the window was open --quietly climbed up on the dumpster. Peaked in, just the two of them, no children. Light the fuse, and drop it through the window. Quick off the dumpster, and walk fast. In the space behind the market it sounded like a 20-gage shot gun going off, the window didn't even come flying out. I gathered the carts and went back in the Market.

Nothing happened for about two hours, everyone just going about their business. The manager's wife showed up and went to the back. She came back and got the head checker. They must have called the assistant manager because when he showed up with his keys, the shit hit the fan. The manager's wife ran out of the back screaming. The head checker was right behind her one hand over her mouth, face whiter than new snow. I got'em -- that's the only thought I had -- I got'em. Things seemed to move real slow, and clear. The assistant manager told me to "stay by the back door and not let anybody go back there --the manager was hurt real bad."

THE TERRORIST

The beat cop showed up first, he was in the office for a few minutes. When he came out, he had blood on his hands and looked sick. The cop got everyone that was still in the market, over in produce well away from the doors. He had another box boy and me on the doors, he told us, “Don't let anyone in,” and to yell really loud if someone tried to leave. Within 30 minutes, there were more police then I had ever seen. Two of them threw up all over the loading dock.

Why I got away, Scot free. with two murders is: the cops thought "Those two assholes belonged dead." The manager had been taking pictures of what they did to little boys. The photographs were in his office storage closet where they died. Every cop from Inglewood, Westchester and El Segundo came to that market sometime in the next three hours.

They stood around in little groups, some even cried. I heard over and over again, “They belong dead.” No one asked me any questions, so it was a surprise, when an El Segundo cop I knew told me my Dad was out front and I could go home. The cop put his hand on my shoulder, like a friend, and walked me out front. That's the day I accepted my different drumbeat and truly began to learn how to march with it.

The market was closed for two day, I spent the time surfing, thinking the whole thing out. I was a murderer by every standard I'd been taught. What was scary? I didn't care one bit. Scarier still, I wanted to tell the whole world, I was proud. I knew the plan had been strong on the get it done side, and weak on the get away with it side --very dangerous. It was time to be cautious, for me that meant, keep my big mouth shut. Not an easy task for a motor mouth.

Most of all, I had to understand lying: how to look someone in the eye and make them believe my lie. That seemed to come naturally to most of you, but then, I was years away from understanding you, me and the human lie.

I went back to work and just acted confused, not a hard task. Everyone else wanted to talk. All I had to say was "Why?" "Do you think so?" "I can't understand," and they were happy to explain. As it turned out, when one of the first cops in the storage closet found the pictures, they were sure it was one of those kids' dad, and I don't think they wanted to catch a dad.

Toward the end of that summer there was a storm, somewhere out in the pacific. That storm generated the best surf of my young life, from Ventura County Line to the tip of Baja California. The surf was 10 to 15 feet of the most perfectly formed waves anyone could remember. Just what a skinny little 15-year-old murderer needed. A gift from God.

The truth of the matter is, I was not a very good surfer. I had the will but not the grace. A good surfer is one with his board and that joint venture does not ride a wave, it dominates it. I could get up on anything, big waves, little waves, no problem, but the wave was boss.

THE TERRORIST

The first day of the storm surf I found a passion and talent, which has stayed with me all these years. Just paddling out, in big surf, takes brass ones the size of basketballs. There is a huge amount of well-grounded fear to overcome. These mountains made of water are trying to pound you directly into the bottom of the sea. That first day I was with Murray Bishop, Skipper Fats and Eddie Jacobsmire, three guys that were one with their boards.

All of us got through the surf line, I was the only one dumb enough to take off on the first wave. It was a 12-foot wall that broke as soon as I was up. It pounded me into the bottom. Worse still, it made me two surfboards. The guys said that the two halves of my board shot about twenty feet in the air. Both halves spinning in opposite directions, they thought it looked bitchin': I was pissed!

After sitting on the beach pouting for a half hour, I got one fin out of Eddie's trunk, and went body surfing. I had seen guys body surf big waves. I had never done it, but to Hell with it, I wasn't going to waste the waves. Good choice. It's the only thing in my life I didn't have to learn the hard way. From the first, I was one with the wave, I belonged there. In my mind that first wave is as clear as this morning. It was a right, breaking from left to right. I was watching the monster approach, looking over my shoulder. One kick with my fin, one pull with my arms, and I was in moving with the wave.

I leaned my right shoulder into the wave, arms at my

side, hands cupped, and cut across the face like a rocket. It was breaking too far behind me, so I cut back and headed toward the break. Just as I entered the tube -- that's the top of a wave just as it breaks over and heads down -- a quick cut back, and I was in the tube. A translucent world that belongs just to those strong enough to get there.

If the wave is perfect and you get yourself in the right position, you can be shot out of the tube, and back into the shoulder of the wave as it breaks. The air being driven out of the tube, as the wave behind you collapses, spits you out. Damn, I came flying out of that tube and back into the slope of the wave in front of me.

Wave after wave everything was perfect. I didn't wipe out once that day. I surfed till I dropped, I had not been out of the water since I got Eddie's fin. I felt strong like a bull, but I needed a drink. Up on the beach, for a quick RC Cola and I'd be back. As I walked up the beach my whole body drained, I dropped to the sand weaker than I had ever been. All I could think was, "Thank you, God. What a day!" When the guys brought me home, I was so whipped Murray helped me carry the pieces of my surfboard to the garage.

Dad came out and was real cool. He knew how hard I had worked to get that board. It wasn't one of the new Styrofoam boards, it was balsa with three mahogany stringers. The board was 9 foot 6 inches, when it had been in one piece. El Segundo's most famous surfer, Velzee, had made it in shop class, before he quit school.

He and Hap Jacobs had opened the first Custom Surfboard Shop. I had gotten it second hand and it was a big status symbol. Dad looked it over and said he was sure we could repair the board. I couldn't see how, but my Dad could build anything. My status symbol would live again.

I ate and was in bed by 7 o'clock, an unheard of hour for me. Eddie was to pick me up at 5 am. There were only a couple times a year that we got big surf and I had never seen better formed waves. Two days left till school, we would use Gods gift to its fullest.

Each of the last two days, we had dragged our dead-tired, pain-racked, skinny little asses north to Zero Beach. As we would stand studying the surf our bodies would fill with energy, and the pain would disappear. If you want it bad enough, nothing matters. Mom had taken a picture of me leaving for school for school. Thank God; there was no timed mile swim the first day. In the picture, I look like the walking dead.

This was my Junior year and I pulled off the most enjoyable crime of my young life to that date. About ninety percent of my crimes were on my own, but a few required help. Most teenage boys are doing one damn crime or another, the problem being, they have to tell everyone, and that is the surest way to get caught.

In high school Leroy, Ron and Tank were my crime buddies. If it required more than me, they were the guys. Not only did they not talk but each was a loner in his own way. Ron and Tank were brothers from a strict Catholic family. If they got caught it was off to Catholic School. We would frequently do a second-story job on the plunge and spend some time skinny dipping.

Leroy was taller and stronger so he would stand on the ledge with his fingers in the thick wire over the girls changing room windows. They always left the second story windows, over the stands, part way open. Leroy would hold on while I climbed his back and got myself standing on his shoulders. My face and chest would be pressed hard against the side of the plunge, my arms, would be stretched over my head reaching for the window ledge. Our combined height left me about six inches short of reaching the ledge.

The next part always had my sphincter muscle pinched tight, sweat running in my eyes and my heart pounding on the plunge wall. It was a leap of faith, bend the knees as much as possible, without FALLING and jump up. My fingers would just grasp the lip of the window sill. Pull myself up, edge the window open and I was in. I would sit in the stands for a couple minutes, let the sphincter loosen, mop the sweat from my face and feel my heart slow down. I would open the back door and we where all in.

El Segundo was a miniature San Francisco, a hill on every street and a street on every hill. In the fifties cars had no steering wheel locks, and in our town, rarely had their doors locked. One night at the plunge, I ran my plan past the guys. I wanted to hide cars, move them from where they should be, to where they couldn't be seen.

Put these facts together with my mind, and there was only one thing to do: late Sunday, early Monday remove as many cars as possible from drive ways, car ports, in front of houses, and place them where the owner couldn't find their car when they tried to leave for work Monday morning. That meant rolling them down a hill and around at least one corner, two if possible. There had to be an out of the way space for parking the car. We didn't want someone calling the cops too early. The guys went for it big.

This one took a lot of planning. We cruised around town checking out parking spots. One market was at the bottom of a long hill on the right, with parking in the back. It was good for ten cars. We could move about fifteen cars from the car ports behind the apartments over looking Imperial Highway, and hide them behind an old warehouse. The rest would be scattered all over town, no more than one or two from any given block.

We started moving cars at eleven thirty pm. Sunday. We hit the car ports first. Next we filled our quota in the market parking lot. Ron and Leroy went one way, Tank and I another. We took turns steering, pushing and being the lookout. The plan called for us to meet at Pat Mars Drive-in, no later then three thirty am. Monday. We had a shake and fries in Leroy's Ford while we talked over our crime. Our total for the night was fifty-seven cars. We went home laughing.

One guy, who was swimming the early morning mile with me said someone stole his dads' car last night. The car thefts were the talk of the school, by lunch time, it was over a hundred cars stolen by a big car theft ring. Our little crime was the biggest thing to hit El Segundo all year.

The local weekly paper had a front page story claiming the police had finger prints of the vandals. I looked up the word vandal, it means, one who willfully defaces or destroys property. We had not defaced, destroyed or even stolen anything out of any of the cars. Hell we even locked the doors when we parked them.

There was no accuracy in the press during the fifties, just as now. I suspect there never has been. The city council had several meetings on how to Stem the Rising Tide of Vandalism. No wonder they never caught us, they didn't even know what we had done, let alone who we were.

I remained just within bounds at school so I could play water polo. I was the goalie and my job was to stop any ball from crossing the plain of the goal. It was best to catch the ball with two hands but you stopped it any way you could. Chest, arms or face anything you could get in front of that very hard, soccer size ball.

The goalie, has a special kick he uses to drive himself out of the water to his waist, and hold himself there with arms spread across the goal. Of course it's called the goalie kick. As the right leg drives down the left comes up, you add an eggbeater motion to each leg and move the legs at a sustained rapped pace. What you get is a lot of power to lift the body out of the water, and block a shot. Oh yes, in water polo you are not aloud to touch the bottom.

That mile we would swim every morning before school, that was not gym, that was our time. Gym for the team was last period of the day and if you wanted to play, you stayed till Coach Sarri said go home.

Practice for me started with a quarter mile goalie kick. I would have ten pounds, in an old ammo belt, around my waist, and hold another ten pounds in my hands. The rest of the team would be swimming fifty-yard wind sprints with the ball. In water polo, you swim with your head out of the water, your arm strokes are not in front of your face, but at shoulder width. The ball is moved down the pool between the arms with your face. The only player that can touch the ball with both hands at once is the goalie.

When we had completed our laps, circles of six or seven were formed and two balls were randomly passed back and forth, till coach blew his whistle. Now the fun began: Scrimmage. When you love to play a game, things are never better than when you play against the best. We were the best.

Teams are not natural to the human, that's why great ones are so rare. They are purposefully forged, hammered into a unit that lifts the individual to a higher level than they could ever hope to attain. El Segundo didn't have the most, the strongest, the fastest, it had Coach Sarri and he forged us into a TEAM.

My junior year I decided, if people were going to give me reasons for things that were obviously bullshit, I would make up my own answers. As is my want,I went for the big answer first. I had never doubted God, but everything people told me about GOD was just so much crap. Dad required us to go to church each week, he didn't care which one, that choice was ours. I started paying close attention and asking questions. I found that most people do not like to be asked questions about God. They get uncomfortable and dogmatic. I went to every church in town that year and they were all the same. They were right and everyone else was going to Hell.

I kept having this strange thought. If God was that shallow and petty, I hoped I would have the courage of my convictions when my turn came to face my maker. Dig my toes in the cloud, look God dead in the eye and give that weak-willed crybaby the finger! I just couldn't see having all that power, and being that petty.

There were some people around who would admit to being atheists. At that time not the in thing to be, but their answers sounded like circle talk to me. When I say circle talk, I mean, it sounds good, the words and phrases all flow -- it's often said with feeling. When you think about what has been said, it starts no where, and ends in the same place.

THE TERRORIST

Circle talk is about ninety present of what passes for public discourse. It took me that whole year, a lot of extra time in the library, pestering religious people all over town, then I found the answer in the damn dictionary. The statement, One All Powerful God, had been banging around in my head all my life, maybe I didn't understand the words. I got the dictionary, started looking the words up, and writing the meanings in a list. One All Powerful God

One: Being a single individual.

All: The entire substance or extent of.

Powerful: Possessing great force.

God: The self-existent and eternal creator , sustain-er, and ruler of life and the universe.

As I read over the meanings of the words, I got mad. It was too simple. If there is One All Powerful God, everything is and of God. There can be nothing else. All the stars, the dog shit in the yard and me were part of God. I don't know why I was mad, maybe it was just too simple and I was a teenager and I was supposed to be mad. One thing for sure, I have never had another misunderstanding of GOD!

"YOU SORRY SACK OF SIBERIAN SNAKE SHIT"

The summer between my junior and senior year, I went to Uncle Ira's' ranch outside of Green River Wyoming. It would be my third and last summer working on the ranch. That year would be different then the first two, my cousin Norris, wouldn't be there. He had been a year older than me and more like a friend then anything else.

He was now dead. Norris had been shot in the stomach Christmas day, the year before and died on the Operating table. His best friend had been showing him his new rifle, of course he had thought it was unloaded. Bam! Norris died two hours later. I had thought about the difference between my two murders and stupidly killing your best friend by accident. If it had been me, that did the shooting, I would have been in total despair.

Uncle Ira was a hard old style man, when he picked me up at the train station, we went straight to the Cemetery. Standing over Norris grave Uncle Ira said "Karl my son died a stupid death! Both of them where raised to know all guns are always loaded. Don't die a stupid death!" With that said he turned and walked back to his truck. The subject of my cousins death was never mentioned again.

Ira's ranch was twenty three miles outside of town on the Green River. The ranch was his seven day a week day job. His night job was only six nights a week, Ira was the yard engineer at the Roundhouse in Green River. He had Thursday night off but worked every day of the week. Every Thursday after noon the two ranchers from further up the river would come to Ira's ranch. He would have a fifty-five-gallon drum in the back of his truck to fill with gas. The three of them would pile in Ira's' truck, drive to town, buy gas and whatever else they needed.

Everyone in Green River new what came next, the Veterans of Foreign Wars, commonly known as the V.F.W. Those three didn't go for any meeting, they went to get drunk and maybe do a little fighting. All three were in the five foot six to five foot nine range, 150 to 160 pounds, no fat and hard as nails. The kids in town said, if they couldn't get anyone else to fight, they fought each other.

On Thursday night just before I went to bed, I was to open the gate to the ranch. Ira said that way he wouldn't forget and drive through the damn thing. His old Ford, looked like it had been through the gate, a few times. I slept on the hay stack above the coral. It is still the finest place I have ever slept. My sleeping bag would sink into the hay like a big soft pillow, the smell of fresh cut alfalfa would fill my head and I could see stars that went on forever, in the night sky.

Early one Friday mourning I lay half awake, hearing my uncle's Ford, the horn blowing, as it wound along the road above the river. **Shit! I had forgotten.** I came up out of my bag and was down off the stack running for the gate. I just crested the hill above the gate when that old Ford went straight through it.

I turned and ran for the barn. I couldn't let him catch me till he slept it off. I could hear Ira, on top of the hay stack, hollering his favorite curse "You sorry sack of Siberian snake shit." The three of them kept up their search, swearing and laughing. After about thirty minutes Aunt Fran came out and told them "Ira you need to go to bed, you two can sleep in the bunk house or go home. Good night." The drunk ranchers did just what they were told. Thank God for strong women.

The cattle were all run on open range during the spring, summer and into the fall. Early fall they had a round up and brought the cattle into the corral. They could feed one hundred and fifty head through the winter. The barn was a hollowed out hill. They had flattened the top of the hill enough to hold two huge stacks of Alfalfa. The barn entrance side of the hill was in the corral, all they had to do was throw Alfalfa of the hill into the corral and the cattle were fed.

Ira had some one-hundred-twenty acres in alfalfa that had to be cut and stacked for winter feed. That took most of my summer, but if you did a man's work you got treated like a man. For a city kid it was big stuff.

Teenagers all over the country had different little regional tricks they got up to; California, midnight auto, swiping car parts; Michigan and Ohio, steal corn and roast it. Anywhere there still had out houses they were pushed over etc. In Green River the crime of choice was called a chick-o-re. The boys went and stole chickens and the girls cleaned and cooked them.

Sounds easy enough, but there are a couple small problems. Chickens are not like hub caps, they make a lot of noise, then there is ROCK-SALT. Rock-salt was part of the ranchers' game. They removed the shot from shotgun shells, and replaced it with rock-salt. Pour some salt in the next wound you get, it will become quickly apparent what the ranchers were up to.

Stealing chickens requires special talents, of which I had none. I was running from the chicken coop with a big hen. Do not wrap your arms around a chicken, hold it to your chest and run. The damn chicken got out of my arms. Do not bend over with arms out stretched trying to catch a running chicken. Better yet do not steal chickens, they're not worth it.

It seemed that the sound and the pain came as one. If you have ever heard a twelve-gage shoot gun speak from the barrel side, up close and personal, you have never forgotten it. The pain was instant. From my ass to ankles, it just seared. All I could do was run screaming shit!, over and over again. The pain does not go away till the rock salt dissolves. One of life's lessons.

I'm sure the rancher had more fun hearing me scream my head off then I had at the Chick-o-Re that night. I had to ride back laying on my belly, in the back of a pick-up truck. All the guys thought it was good for the surfer boy to get a taste of the rock salt.

To this day I believe it was a set up. The two guys I was with didn't go in with me. One of them drove us out there, and the other showed me how to get to the chicken coop, just over the hill from the old dirt road we were on. He was waiting at the top of the hill when I came running by screaming shit. At least they hadn't run out on me.

Two days later I had to tell Aunt Fran what happened. My ass and the back of my legs were infected. The rock salt had taken little pieces of my 5O1's and buried them under my skin. The rock salt had dissolved, the little pieces of 501 never would. My first tattoo.

There was a working dog on the ranch, called Jake by everyone but Ira. He never spoke to the dog, just pointed and Jake did what Ira wanted. If you saw Ira, the dog was close. Jake was smarter then most people and was full of courage.

Ira had sent me up the river, to repair some fence, that kept cattle from going up a dry wash. I had gathered my tools, saddled up and ridden about a quarter mile. There was a gate in the fence line, on a hill that over looked the ranch. I passed through the gate, when I swung back up on my horse, I could see the whole ranch. Ira was standing by the work shed with Jake sitting about ten feet away. Ira pointed up at me and Jake was off like a shot, running fast and low little puffs of dust flying of his feet. How did that dog know what was on Ira's mind?

We had about an hour ride. I felt like king of the world, a good horse, a saddle gun and a great dog. What more could a sixteen year old ask. When we got to the dry wash, all three strands of the fence, were down. Jake started acting strange right away, he didn't bark, he got antsy. His nose was to the ground, running back and forth, Jake would look up the dry wash then back at me.

As I sat there, watching that dog wondering what he was trying to tell me, the most god awful sound came out of the wash. I had that special thought, I get when things are out of my control: SHIT. There is only one thing in the world that made that sound -- Hereford bulls challenging each other for control of the herd.

I was not going up that wash, between fifteen to twenty foot walls of dirt, I defiantly was not king. Jake took charge, he ran up the hill by the mouth of the wash, turned and looked at me. Hey good idea, I followed, at least I wouldn't be setting right in front of their only exit, waiting to get trampled.

Two hundred feet up the wash, it made a ninety degree turn, and widened from twenty feet to about seventy. The combatants were Ski Foot, Ira's prize Hereford bull and one I didn't recognize. They were bellowing, pawing the dirt and generally acting like a couple guys getting ready to fight. I could see a bunch of heifers, further up the wash.

Jake had it all thought out, as soon as he had me up and out of the way, he took off running fast. Down a cut in the side of the wash, straight for the bulls. If you've never seen a Hereford bull up close, just think a ton of fast muscle with horns. Jake on the other hand was about 40 pounds of mongrel dog, but it took him less than a very scary minute, to turn both bulls and have them headed out of the wash.

When I got back to the mouth of the wash, Ski Foot was just across the downed fence and Jake was running the strange bull toward the river. It only took a couple hours to bring those pretty little cows the bulls were ready to kill for out of the wash, and repair the fence.

Ira, Jake and I spent four days scouting the herd and eating what we shot. We brought coffee and a little flour for biscuits. Sage chicken and jack rabbit were everywhere. If you couldn't shoot'em, you didn't deserve to eat. Ira is a quiet man and even my motor mouth took a rest. You heard the saddle against the horse, hooves on ground, brush on hide and on occasion the crack of a rifle.

Few words were exchanged. Ira read sign, the record all animals leave in their surroundings as they pass. When he wanted me to check something, he would point at me, point two fingers at his eyes, then point where he wanted me to go. Ira always sent Jake with me. He knew the dog would keep me out of trouble.

Ranches are nonstop work, so a little ride, locating

cattle is like a paid vacation. We found a heifer stuck in the mud, put a rope on her and pulled her out. When Ira didn't like where we found cattle, he would point at the cattle and point the direction he wanted them to go, Jake would move them out. All easy stuff.

I had been allowed to bring only nine rounds for the old 22 pump rifle I carried. Ira said, "Make your shots count or you don't eat. Hunger is a good teacher." He was right, it took me just four wasted shoots, and one night with no food. My flighty young brain focused, I didn't waste another shot. Jack rabbits, on the run, are not an easy shot. On the other hand, sage chickens are a big, dumb bird, slow to fly. I shot sage chicken and ate.

We spent the last night with an old Basque sheepherder Ira liked. The old man had given him Jake, years before, as a puppy. Late that afternoon, Ira shot a small antelope and brought it to the old man. His camp was fancy, compared to what ours had been. The old man had a horse drawn wagon he lived in, two horses and three dogs. He and his dogs would move the sheep around an area till they had grazed it out, then move the camp and flock to a new area.

The Old Man and Ira went to work and fixed a meal for fit for kings. They stuffed the sage chicken with wild onions and herbs, from down by the river, put it in a covered pot and slow cooked it at the side of the fire. They dressed the antelope and spit roasted the round.

My job was to turn the spit, baste the round with mutton fat and catch what drippings I could in a small pan. Every ten minutes or so I would pour half the drippings over the antelope, then lift the lid on the pot and pour the rest over the sage chicken. We were the Kings and we ate.

That night Ira talked more then I had ever heard. He and the Old Man swapped stories around the fire. I lay back on my bedroll with a stuffed belly and just listened. When I feel asleep, the Old Man was singing, low and sweet. Ira said the old man was ninety years old, that meant he had been born in eighteen hundred and sixty eight. The Basque people come from an area in both Spain and France. They have their own language and know more about sheep than anyone.

That summer was a respite, from my headlong plunge, toward the end of puberty. I had restored my supply of sullen glances, smart ass remarks, sneers and general lack of common sense. I told no one my goal: stay in school till after water polo season, then get kicked out and join the Navy. In the fifties and sixties, unlike today, you could be in all kinds of trouble and still get in the Navy. In all truth, if I had just behaved myself and asked my folks, they would have let me quit school and join the Navy. That was just too easy.

THE TERRORIST

The Big Lie and a Bad Kill

The Navy Recruiter had his office in Inglewood . He always had time to see young guys and answer your questions. As it turned out he was just one of those people that would smile and tell you anything you wanted to hear. His lies to me would cost him his life. First Class Gunners Mate Gary D. Fine was to become my first, thought out, premeditated murder. You might say: Gathering tools for things to come.

Petty Officer Fine told me, "Just do well in boot camp, if you do they will send you straight to Underwater Demolition Team Training ." Major lie. At that time, you could join the Navy at seventeen with your parent's consent, but could not be accepted in training, for Underwater Demolition Teams, until you were twenty-one and had served one year in the fleet. His lie could cost me four years of my life.

I had turned seventeen in November, we won the state championship in December. By January my parents were happy to sign the papers. Boot Camp was no sweat for me. I had been away from home many times and a lot of what they were trying to teach us I had learned from Mom, Dad and the Boy Scouts.

Most of the guys had never been away from home. I was the only guy in my Company that could sew and well over half couldn’t make their own bed. Swimming. A full third of our guys couldn't pass the Navy’s basic, and I do mean basic, swim tests. My Company Commander made me Athletic Petty Officer and told me "Every man passes the swim test in one month or you don't graduate." Heavy pressure for a seventeen-year-old, but I'm sure it helped me respond to the challenge.

In boot camp the companies were all in competition, trying to gain points and little colored pennants that you hung on your company flag. Having non-swimmers cost you points. A non-swimmer could not graduate from boot camp and that would cause your Company Commander to loose status.

The Company Commanders took their status seriously and could cause any recruit who didn't comply endless misery. For most of these guys it was the first time mommy and daddy were not there to shield them from the bad ass world. Most of boot camp was Mickey Mouse, but you better take it seriously.

I didn't find out that I had been lied to, about UDT training, till the last week of boot camp so I busted butt, some might say kissed ass, on every task. I did find out that I'm a good teacher. Everyone in our company could pass his swim test after two weeks. The Brigade Commander passed down orders that I was to be assigned to the pool, every day for two hours, and assist the other company's non-swimmers in passing their test. My Company Commander viewed this as status enhancement. I was his boy.

THE TERRORIST

If I know it, I can teach it, but I have to get right in the middle of whatever the subject is. The Navy Instructors sat everyone down, would do a little demo, then expect everyone to learn. They would stand on the edge of the pool, blowing their whistles, and shouting. That method may work for most, but some people can't learn that way. I started every session with all my non-swimmers setting on the edge of the pool, and me in the water. I would then swim for laps, breaststroke, one hundred yards' underwater. When I had my breath back, I would swim two laps breaststroke, on the surface, with one of the non-swimmers on my back.

After my little demo they would believe me when I said, YOU WILL PASS THE TEST, NO PROBLEM! When one guy had any type of success, I would have him show everyone, if it was just holding their face under water. I would then be pair him with one guy who couldn't hold his face underwater. Each guy trying to show, teach, the next. I would jump around from guy to guy, little group to little group, trying to teach everyone. Whenever you try to teach another, you learn more yourself.

Our Company Commander was a Chief Boatswain Mate with tattoos all over his body. He had an eyeball in the middle of his forehead, hula girls on his ear lobes, chains around his neck, wrist and ankles. The man was big, talked in a loud deep voice and had everyone convinced, he was pure mean. He showed up at the pool one day, with the strangest little kid I had ever seen. He looked like he had been made out of rejected parts. He had a face from some foreign place, his body was squat, his arms were too long and his legs were too short. He was a mongoloid and my Company Commander's adopted son. They loved each other.

I had just finished swimming my underwater, show off laps and was hanging onto the edge of the pool gasping for breath. I looked up and locked eyes with the kid, he was sitting on a bench, on his dad's lap. There were ten non-swimmers that day, and they all looked scared shitless. For some reason, the strange kid with his eyes locked on mine and arms around that big bad-assed guy's neck, made me smile. The kid had a big silly grin on his face, he brought one arm down and waved to me. I started laughing and choking all at once, I waved back.

That day at the pool, when I quit choking and laughing, the Chief smiled. I had never seen him smile. He said they would meet me out front when I was done with the class. The three of us sat on the steps in front of the pool. The kids' name was Bobby but the Chief called him Boats, short for Boatswain Mate.

The Chief had always told me, he had never asked. That day he was asking. Boats was seven years old and had damn near drowned the year before. They had tried everything they could think of -- teach themselves, private swim class, several of the Navy instructors. Would I try and teach Boats to swim? The Chief had cleared it with Battalion Headquarters. If I tried there would be no favor returned. If I didn't want to try, or Boats didn't learn to swim there would be no problem.

THE TERRORIST

I didn't know what to think. Boats was at the top of the steps, running back and forth. I got up and went up the steps to find out if he liked me. If he didn't like me there wasn't a chance. I just held out my arms, Boats looked at me, stooped forward, and came running. His little short legs were bowed, so running was more a lurch from side to side. When he got to me he jumped up and threw his arms around my neck. Damn, he was heavy and solid as a rock, his arms were so strong that as he hugged me, it felt like he could break my neck.

The surprise must have shown on my face, Chief laughed, shook his head and said "Don't be fooled, Boats is a lot more then he looks like". It was strange, Boats made me feel good, like my brother. I asked him if he could talk, he shook his head up and down. I asked if he could learn to swim, again he shook his head up and down. So I said; "Boats if you want me to teach you to swim you say the word yes." Boats shook his head up and down and said yes.

"Chief if you will take Boats and the whole company to the Gi-dunk, the day he passes his Basic Navy swim test, I don't see how they could call that giving favor." Chief just looked at Boats and me for a while, and said, "Done."

Chiefs and where they fit in the Untied States Navy, needs to be explained. Not becoming a chief is the worst failure of my life. They are the hinge pin, which holds that huge war machine together. You could eliminate any other rate or rank, Seaman Recruit to

Admiral and the Navy would sail on. Eliminate Chiefs and the Navy sinks, like a ship with its bottom ripped out.

They know every man's job, where he fits and how to use him. They stand between the Officer and the lower ranks. They send up what's needed, and down what to do. If they like you they can protect you from anyone but God. They are the men that float that vast gray murder machine, which stays between you and the bad guys. Our Company Commander was my first Chief, and he set a high standard, for those that followed over the next nine years. In my mind, he is always, THE CHIEF.

I don't know if my teaching Boats to swim ever saved his life, but three months down the road his love saved me from suffering the consequences of a murder I regret to this day. Boats learned to swim but never passed the Basic Navy Swim test. You had to be able to float to pass the test and I couldn't teach Boats to float. He was solid muscle, no fat, any time he tried to float, Boats went straight to the bottom. They call it negative buoyancy. To this day I have never seen anyone as negative as Boats. He sank like a lead anchor.

We had use of the pool for three hours, on Sunday after church. The Chief would sit way up in the back of the stands and do paperwork. Boats and I had the water all to ourselves. He loved riding around the pool on my back and watching me swim under water. It took me half the first lesson to teach him not to chock me when I swam with him on my back.

THE TERRORIST

Riding me seemed to be Boats idea of swimming, so we made a deal. Every time Boats learned something I gave him a ride around the pool. Mongoloids read people in a different way, somehow they quickly know if you accept them. If you do, they will give you everything. Over the years I have observed, the only things they are truly greedy about have to do with food and love.

The chief and his wife had Boats practice breaststroke every night for fifteen minutes. They would place him, face down on a big pillow. One would work his arms, the other his legs. Breaststroke is the most powerful stroke, not the fastest but powerful like a tugboat. It was the stroke I used to swim with someone on my back. The stroke takes timing, you pull with your arms, then kick as your arms recover. Both arms must pull and recover like a mirror image, the legs must do the same. We hoped Boats could get the timing right, with his Mom and Dad guiding his arms and legs, over and over.

While I was teaching Boats, he was teaching me. Boats knew every nautical term and every bit of Navy slang there was. His favorite Gi-dunk, that's where you went to get Pogi-bait, ice cream, candy and the like. Deck, the floor. Leak my Lizard, take a piss. Bow, the front of a ship. Stern the back of a ship. Port, the left side of a ship while looking at the bow, if you look to the stern, port is on your right. Starboard, looking to the bow, the right side of a ship. Climb in my tree, go to bed. The brig, jail. The head, where you went to leak your lizard. As you can see the Navy has its own language, if you don't know the language, slang and all, you don't fit. Old Salt, a sailor who has been around a long time. Boats made me sound like an Old Salt.

It only took three weeks for Boats to swim the length of the pool. He could make a life jacket out of his pants and hold his breath, underwater, for one minute. If he stopped swimming, he was still on the bottom like an anchor. The deal had been pass the Basic Navy Swim test, no float, no pass. The Chief and his wife were so damn happy that Boats could swim, they paid off anyway. The fourth Sunday, his mom, his three sisters and my whole company showed up at the pool.

Boats did his stuff and the guys were great. Every time Boats showed them something he had learned, they would clap their hands, stomp their feet on the wooden deck of the stands and chant Boats, Boats, Boats. He loved it, shit, we both loved it. When we finished showing off in the pool, Boats and I felt nine feet tall.

The Chief and his wife took everyone to the Gi-dunk. There was a big enclosed area behind the main building that was all set up for a party. She and the girls, Patty age fourteen, Susan age twelve, and Judith Jo age eleven and a half, had baked three big sheet cakes. One was decorated with a swimming pool and said "BOATS SWIMS." There were three big containers of ice cream and two big platters of home made chocolate chip cookies. All the Pogi-bait any young sailor could want.

The Chief and the Brigade Commander had on Dress

Whites, swords and all. They called everyone to attention, brought Boats to the head table and presented him with a trophy. It had his name, BOATS and one word, SWIMMER.

It was the first time in my life that I laughed and cried at the same time, I had big tears running down my cheeks and was laughing so hard I couldn't stand to attention. Little Judith Jo looked up at me with those big brown eyes, took my hand and helped me sit down. She crawled up in my lap, put her little arms around my neck and said "We love you."

She looked just like Natalie Wood in Miracle on 36th Street. I didn't know then but she had taken my heart for life. Life is good, such simple things loom so large in my life. I would have it no other way. The Chief looking like some ancient mighty warrior, Boats sitting on his shoulders, walked around the party quietly talking with each man. How, could a man with an eyeball tattooed in the middle of his forehead have so damn much dignity?

Judith Jo sat on my lap watching her Dad move from man to man, her mom and sisters serving cake and ice cream. She was a serious person at eleven years old, self possessed, inquisitive, her big brown eyes looked straight in yours when she talked or listened to what you had to say. She asked me if I was married, about my mom, dad and brothers. Judith Jo said "If I didn't already know how to swim, I would have you teach me". Sitting there all I could think was, Thank you Lord, a perfect day.

Funny what twenty-four little hours can do, one day at peace with the world, the next my soul seething with hatred, bent on murder. When I finished at the pool on Monday the Chief was waiting for me outside. He was all military, "Airman Recruit Austin, I've been looking into Underwater Demolition Team Replacement Training, and you're not eligible. Applicants must be twenty-one years of age, upon receipt of Order to Underwater Demolition Team Training, you are seventeen!"

I have no idea what happened over the next hour. I was numb to everything outside of myself. Just before formation I was leaning against our scrub table, where we washed our clothes. You were not supposed to sit or lean on a scrub table. The Recruit Chief Petty Officer from the Company next to ours walked by and told me to get my ass off the table.

Now, Recruit Chief Petty Officer sounds like a big deal but he's just another recruit. I don't remember if I heard him or not but when he started pulling on my arm, I was on him like stink on a garbage can. I didn't like him anyway. He was one of those guys that will step on people whether he has to or not. That day he was the one stepped on.

When they got me off him, both his eyes were swelling and his uniform was ripped to shit. What saved my ass from going to the brig, was our clothes line watch -- yes we had guards on the clothes lines. Anyway the guard liked me. I had taught him to swim so he lied just a little, and made it sound like the Recruit Chief Petty Officer had been jerking hard on my arm before I hit him.

I lost Athletic Petty Officer rank and had to walk four hours Dimsee dumpster watch, guard the trash, every night four a week. I would not find out the full story for years, not until after the Chief had died. Keeping me out of the Brig had cost the Chief as well! He had done a lot of under the table dealing to get me off light.

The Recruit Chief Petty Officer's Company Commander liked the suck-ass. Chief stood three weekend duties for the other Company Commander, so he wouldn't push for me to go to the brig. He called in a few favors and got me orders to my next duty station, where I would be watched over by one of the senior Chief Warrant Officers in the Navy, C.W.O.4 Pappy Hayford. All this I would find out years later, what I knew then was, the Chief was pissed.

He had me in his office for three hours standing in front of his desk at parade rest. He didn't say a word, he didn't even look at me. What he finally said to me was short and sweet. I wasn't ready to hear it then -- I probably never will be. "Grow up Austin, you can't have everything you want." My mind had a will of its own. I guess the closest explanation is, not knowing how to overcome myself. I still had not learned I was my own worst friend. God Bless your enemies, You always know where they stand. Bad friends catch you unaware.

John Carl Roat

My own bad friend

For three hours I had stood there and thought about nothing but Petty Officer First Class Fine, and how I would kill him while I was home on Boot Camp leave.

As it turned out the ship I received orders to, an aircraft carrier named Saratoga, was home ported in Long Beach California, just thirty miles from my objective. So I took a little more time to get the job done. As you will see murder, like any other high risk endeavor, requires both skill and luck. If you don't have the luck, you will never gain the skills. I have the luck so I gained the skills.

I like doing crime alone. I have since childhood. Every crime I have committed against the people of the United States is mine alone. The people I admire enough to work with, would not do what I have done. To top it off, now that they know it's me, they think I've gone crazy, and are doing their best to help catch my ass. Well I am crazy, crazy enough to have gotten away with stopping huge segments of this country, by myself. Maybe, just maybe, my crazy thought processes are better then yours. Think about it.

Sorry, I'm stalling. This murder is one of few things in my life that I am truly ashamed of. First Class Petty Officer Fine did not deserve to die. Plus, I did a shit job of it. Not like I didn't have a lot of planning time.

El Segundo, Inglewood and Long Beach are close to

each other, in the Los Angles California area. El Segundo and Inglewood butt right up to each other. It was no problem following Fine around, discovering where he lived, his hang outs, what his schedule was, etc. I spent a good part of my two-week Boot Camp leave as Fine's unseen shadow. The cops would have never come up with my name if I had been smart enough to keep it that way.

The second weekend I was home I spent a day with a couple friends body-surfing at a place called the Wedge. After a day of good surf, hot sun, and plenty of beer we went to a place in Inglewood called Scarpaleanos. It was a huge pizza place, with plenty of young girls, and a friend who would slip us pitchers of beer. In those days you had to be twenty-one to drink, or vote, but you could kill people for your nation, at seventeen.

I knew Fine sometimes came in to eat, and should have stayed clear of the place, especially when I had been drinking. I have little inhibition without booze. When I was drinking I had none. I was sitting at the corner of a long table in the back room when Fine came in. As he walked by our table, he stopped looked down, gave a little smirk and said "How's it going, Frogman."

I called him some name as I started up off the bench. Not smart. He hit me half way up. I bounced off the people behind me and onto their table. He got me again as I got off the table, this time I went to the floor. It was a crowded room and people were trying to get out of the way. I was stepped on, pushed and kicked. I remember looking up from the floor and seeing Fine with a big smile on his face.

In all the confusion my friends got us out of there. Good guys, they could have just hauled ass and left me. By the time we got down the street to my station wagon, both my eyes were swollen damn near shut and I had a big knot on the side of my head. The next morning everything was worse; I was hung over and beat up, my body hurt where people had stepped on me, and my mom wanted to know "What the hell happened?"

I had to lie. There are two methods of lying, that sometimes work for me. 1) Tell a whopper. This takes a lot of planning, generally this method should be used on those that don not know you well. It works best on large groups, ask any politician. 2) Keep as close to the truth as possible, and try to have someone, who will be cosigner for your story. This method has its best success rate on those that know you well. I chose number two, I told her everything except who. Fine became some stranger.

Even a young stupid guy, like me, knew I couldn't kill Fine this week and hope to get away with it. My plan was simple, I do like simple! Fine had an apartment over a hardware store about two blocks from the Navy Recruiters office. He parked his car in the alley behind the store. The entrance to his apartment was at the top of a set of exposed stairs going up the back of the building. The stairs where lit by one light bulb, over the landing at the top of the stairs. He lived alone and went drinking every night. All things that should make his murder an easy crime to get away with.

Sometime around 12:00 P.M., a half hour either way, he would park his car in a small space between the Hardware, and the Furniture Emporium next store. Walk about thirty feet to the stairs, going up the back of the Hardware Store to his Apartment. The only light for half a block either way, was on the landing, at the top of his stairs.

I had removed the light bulb one night and watched to see what he would do. He parked, damn near running into the big trash bin at the rear of the Emporium, I was hiding in the bin. Fine got out of his car muttering and took a leak on the wall of the Hardware. He staggered a little going up the stairs, opened the door and went in his apartment.

I had bought a nine shoot 22 revolver, double action, with a 6-inch barrel and two boxes of ammo, from a surfer I knew. He sold guns under the table, no questions ask, cash only. The gun and I had been to the sand dunes to make sure we worked well with each other, there was no problem, I was ready.

My plan was simple, at 10:45 P.M. park three blocks away, straight down the alley at a 24-hour Drive-in. Walk to Fines place, if his car wasn't there, unscrew the landing light, lay down on the landing and wait. When he walked up the stairs and his head was level with the edge of the landing, shoot him in the face. It should only take one shot,

I was using 22 longs and his face would be about six to seven to feet from the end of the barrel. With Fine in the middle of the stairs, I'd have time for more shots if I missed the first. Then down the stairs, a quick check of Fine and throw the revolver in the trash bin. Walk down the alley, removing my rubber gloves, place in pocket for later disposal. I had never touched the revolver or rounds without gloves. At the first corner, come out of the alley onto the main drag, walk to the drive-in and go to the inside counter for a Milk Shake. I didn't want to walk right to my vehicle, better to buy something and not look out of place. Dump the cloves and the long sleeve shirt, one at a time, on the way back to good old El Segundo.

Fine would have to wait, someone, maybe my two friends would remember him kicking my ass. I put everything on hold and went down to San Diego, Boats had invited me to go to the Zoo with him and the rest of his family. It was my last day of leave. I was to report aboard the Saratoga by 1600, 4:00 P.M., the following day.

Chief was out front, mowing the yard, when I found their home. I had never been to the chief's house, and had never seen him in civilian clothes. Somehow it didn't seem right, the Chief in civies. When I got out of my surfer wagon, Chief started laughing and said looks like you have had a good leave. It finally dawned on me, he meant my black eyes. Judith Jo was first out the door with Boats hot on her tail. When she got close enough to see my face, her mouth feel open, and she got big tears in her eyes. Judith Jo thought I was hurt really bad, and it scared her. It took about thirty minutes to get her calmed down, so we could go to the zoo.

We had a great day at the San Diego Zoo. Judith Jo took charge that little girl knew the zoo, and the animals in it. She had been there twenty times and was well known by the Zoo staff. All day she had me by the hand, my personal tour guide, telling me things I didn't know. If I had a question she couldn't answer, she would say "I don't know, but I'll find out." Judith Jo would then proceed to find one of the zoo staff, and get the answer to the question.

Boats spent the day on his Dads big shoulders. He held onto the Chiefs ears, and guided him with gentle little tugs. He was in love with the otters, three times that day he used the Chiefs ears to guide us to the otter pond. Each time he would ask Judith Jo to tell him about the Otters. When she would finish telling us everything she knew, Boats would say, "Boats can swim, Boats is a otter!" There was no doubt Boats was king of the family, and that was how the whole family wanted it.

By the end of the day Boats had not walked fifty steps. He had been on his Dads shoulders, steering him by his ears, back and forth, all over the zoo. As soon as we reached the car he curled up in my lap and went to sleep. At the drive-in I tried to wake him, while his Mother ordered our food. Patty said "Boats won't wake up, but he'll eat" and she giggled. Susan reached over and tickled Boats, he didn't move.

Susan, Patty, Boats and I were in the back seat, Boats on my lap. Patty and Susan had a discussion on how we were going to eat. When the food came Patty would remove the food from the tray, Susan would feed Boats and me, Patty would feed Susan and herself. Judith Jo wanted to feed Boats and me our French Fries over the front seat, her sisters agreed. We decided that they would wait till Boats was fed to feed me. Famous last Orders from the Chief, the voice of authority "Be careful back there, I do not want a mess in this car!"

They were a well-oiled team, it was fun watching the girls feeding Boats and each other. He was like some King, laid back against my chest, food and drink presented to his lips. When he wanted, he ate or drank, when he didn't want food his lips would not move. If one of the girls, playing with him, removed the food from his lips, Boats would give a deep grunt, his royal sign of displeasure.

When he wanted no more Boats put his cheek against my chest and snuggled in. The whole time the girls fed Boats, the deep slow breathing of sleep was only interrupted while he chewed and swallowed. It was the damnedest thing, he ate a hamburger, fries, drank a coke and never woke up.

I was in a silly mood and had been laughing since we got in the car. I'm sure the girls were showing off a little but there had been no mess as yet. When Susan and Judith Jo started feeding me, our success at following the Chiefs Orders quickly evaporated. Susan brought my cheese burger to my lips, as I opened my mouth to bite she pulled back, Boats grunted. Everyone stopped what they were doing and looked at Boats. Their Mother said "Susan, please do that again."

The burger came to my lips, I opened my mouth the burger withdrew, Boats grunted. The chiefs mouth slowly opened and just kept hanging there. I think the sight of the ancient warrior, tattooed eyeball in the middle of his forehead, and mouth hanging open, is what did me in. After a couple experiments, Judith Jo wanted to try with the French-fries.

I finely got a bite of my cheese burger. Susan put the straw of my milk shake to my lips, after I took a sip, I looked up and there was Chief, his mouth still hanging open, and that damned eyeball, staring at me. I started laughing and choking at the same time, burger and strawberry milk shake shooting out of my mouth. The girls were all laughing, Judith Jo leaning over the front seat, spilled the fries all over Boats and me. Susan promptly dumped the milk shake all over us. Chief is hollering "knock it off, knock it off." No one was paying any attention.

Even his wife, leaning over the seat trying to stop the mess in progress, spilled what was left of patties Coke, and she started laughing. I almost regained control of myself, then I looked down at Boats, still sound a sleep, with food and drink all over himself, I was back in laughter land, this time Chief lost it to. It makes me laugh too this day. We must have looked like a car full of nuts. My Stomach hurt for three days, from laughing so hard.

The Chief and I cleaned up their car before I left for home. While we were away from the women, I was trying to find out what kind of problem Petty Officer Fine could cause me about our one-sided fight, without using his name. Chief said "Karl, If you have something on your mind? Spit it out, I can't tell what I'm being asked hear."

I told him what had happened, at Scarpaleanos with Fine. Of course nothing of my plan, just our accidental meeting. Chief said "First, don't bad mouth someone that is standing over you. Second, if it happened like you say, he can't cause you any problems, but if you have witnesses, you could get him Court Marshaled. He would be at least busted in Rank and maybe Brig time. If that's what you want, I'll help you?"

No thanks Chief, as long as he can't mess with me, I don't think I like Court Marshals. Chief said "Good, leave it, lay." Dumb me, I figured nobody in San Diego would hear about a murder way up in Inglewood, hell it was more then ninety miles' away.

I helped tuck the kids in, thanked everyone and

headed for home. The next day I was to report to my first duty station, not what I canted but I was still excited. I had gone down to Long beach twice, while home on leave, to see the Saratoga. Both times I had just stood on the pier. The ship, this man made thing, exuded more power sitting still, doing nothing, than I had ever felt. It was like some poised monster, a beautiful monster that could say only one thing, DO NOT FUCK WITH ME. If I couldn't get my shot at being a Frogman for another four years, this looked like the place to be.

When a new Recruit right out of Boot Camp reports aboard, you're lost. The Navy has a tried and true system, to get you up to speed, and make you functioning part of the crew, A.S.A.P., as soon as possible. You know how to report aboard a ship, they teach you that in Boot Camp, from then on it is a learning buy repetitive practice situation

I reported aboard the After Brow, the Forward Brow is for Officers. You first face the stern of the ship come to attention and Salute the Ensign, our Flag, do an about face and Salute the Petty Officer of the Watch and say, "Airman Apprentice Austin reporting aboard for duty Sir."

They always give a new guy the old up and down look, what do we have here? You are sent down to the Personnel Department, they take charge of your sealed personal file, and send you to your Division. Most guys right out of Boot Camp, go to what is called, I

Division. There you are given time to learn the ship by participating in the dread Navy ritual, the Working Party.

I Division is nothing but a day labor pool that takes care of as many shit jobs around the ship as possible. The Second Class Yeoman that handled my service jacket said "You're not a designated striker and you're none rated, why aren't you going to I Division?" Hell I didn't know anything! He seemed quite upset and made several calls. Then he was really pissed off "What the hell is going on in this mans Navy?" It seems not only did I have a Division assignment, but a T.A.D., Temporary Additional Duty, assignment to something called Side Cleaning Division.

People who live by paper work do not like anyone that doesn't fit their paper work. This guy did not like me. His last call he told someone to, "come get this asshole, I don't know what to do with him." I had been on the ship thirty minutes, said only yes sir, no sir, I don't no sir and had collected my first enemy.

In the Navy, people who work on aircraft are called Airedales, and on Aircraft Carriers they live just under the flight deck. These huge gray killing machines vibrate and pulse with power just setting at the pier. When they are in operation, they assault all your senses and every cell in your body. You learn to sleep with large aircraft slamming into the flight deck a couple feet over your head. More important, you learn to survive and get work done in one of the most dangerous work places in the world, the flight deck.

As you will see, my nine years, six mouths and twenty four days in the worlds largest nuclear canoe club, fit no pattern the Navy had in mind. My first day aboard the U.S.S. Saratoga CVA 60 would be no different. I was taken up to a coffee locker off the starboard catwalk just under the edge of the flight deck. I was turned over to First Class Petty Officer J. D. Gripe. J. D. was the senior Petty Officer for V-4 Division, responsible for all aspects of Aviation Fuel. Getting it aboard, storing it and delivering it, into the aircraft fuel tanks safely. It's not an easy job, along side the pier, underway things are much more difficult. He was the only First Class to head up a Division on the ship. Every other Division had a Chief.

V-4 Division not only didn't have a Chief, it didn't have a Line Officer, Commissioned by Congress. The Division had Pappy Hayford, Chief Warrant Officer W-4, a gift from God. I guess they told us about Warrant Officers in Boot Camp, if they did, it wasn't done right. Lets see if I can do a better job of explaining what a C.W.0.-4 is.

There are more Admirals in the United States Navy then Chief Warrant Officer W-4s. You must move up thirteen pay grades from Recruit, E-l, to C.W.0.-4 It is the highest non-commissioned pay grade in all the United States military. Those are the facts, they don't tell the story. The story is, when the Captain of the Saratoga addressed Pappy Hayford he would say, "Pappy Hayford Sir." Many times I heard, from the

Captain on down, "Pappy Hayford, what do you think, Sir?" No man achieves the rank of Chief Warrant Officer W-4, without being a vast depository of practical knowledge, that he can readily apply. They are men among men, and are treated with great respect. To top it all off, they know where all the bodies are buried, and when to use that knowledge. If you have a Chief Warrant Officer W-4 in your corner, you win. I didn't know it at the time but I would have a C.W.O.-4 in my corner. Pappy Hayford would save my ass from jail, and get me my chance at being a Frogman

J. D. set me down, offered me a cup of coffee and laid out what would be expected of me. I would be assigned to Side Cleaners, but unlike most people that are T.A.D., I would return to my V-4 Division duties when the ship was at Air Quarters. J.D. said that if Pappy ask me a question, there was no quicker way to get on his shit list then to try to cover my ignorance with a lot of words. Give him a strait answer, if I didn't know, say, I Don't know Sir. J. D.'s. Personal shit list, started with the name of anyone, who did not show respect to Pappy Hayford. Followed closely by duty shirkers, thieves and malcontents. I would be bunking in the V-4 compartment, and have an extra locker in the coffee mess.

J.D. introduced me to Petty Officer Third Class Wolf, and Airman Good. These were the guys that would get me settled in, show me the ship, and teach me my Air Quarters duties. Wolf and Good first showed me the most important place on the ship, the main Galley,

FOOD. The Saratoga had the main galley, two other enlisted mess decks for when the Squadron was aboard, the First Class mess, the Chiefs mess, and the Wardroom where officers dined.

While we ate, my two new shipmates filled me in on my duties, and the ships scuttlebutt, gossip. Wolf would tell me about our duties, Good would shake his head up and down, cosigning what Wolf said. Good would then tell me some scuttlebutt and Wolf would shake his head up and down cosigning Good.

These two guys made me smile every day, I have never seen a friendship like theirs. Wolf was blond haired, Blue eyed, six foot plus, one hundred and sixty or so pounds and calm at all times. Good was black haired, brown eyed, a squat, thick heavy muscled five nine two hundred pounds, and strung tight as a drawn bow string. Arrow ready to fly.

I never saw a time when they were in disagreement about anything. If one lead, the other followed, neither was always in charge. I never figured out how they determined who lead when. it was like these two vary different people were one strange organism. Hell they lad only known each other six months before I meet them.

They told me the ship had been out of dry dock for three weeks, and we would be doing Sea Trials and short little shake down cruises for the next couple of months. Then West Pack, a seven month cruise, Pearl

Harbor, Sasbo Japan, Hong Kong, Subic Bay Philippines, and Kie Lung Taiwan where the Liberty Ports.

My murder plan popped straight up in my brain. Perfect. Shoot that bastard Fine, and sail out of the country for seven months. Fine was never far from my thoughts, I still had black eyes to remind me. My problem was I still had not mastered critical thinking and wouldn't for many years. It should have been obvious that I would be at least looked at closely. After all, he had kicked my ass in public.

The next day I reported to Side Cleaning Division. Yea, just what it sounds like, keep the ship looking good. There were forty-four sailors in the side cleaning gang. We chipped and scraped paint off the ship, then we put it back. Side Cleaning Division was responsible for the external skin of the Saratoga, remaining rust free and Navy gray. The Division came under the ships First Lieutenant. The way things worked on tile Saratoga, if the ship didn't look good the Executive Officer, X.O , would be all over the First Lieutenant. OF course, the First Lieutenant would fall on us like a ton of shit, NO LIBERTY, and long hours.

Side cleaners was made up of others Divisions nonessential personnel, rejects, new guys etc., etc. Let us just say, the First Lieutenant didn't have the finest tools to get the job done. What he did have, was Whillie, a huge block of human malevolence, and Hartso, six foot three of v shaped mussel. Hartso had a teeny little head, that housed a teeny little brain. He would do anything that Whillie told him, even if God said no. The ship stayed clean on terror and terror alone.

After Quarters each mourning, Hartso would break us up in groups, and give us to the Riggers. That's the guys who rigged stages and nets so we could work on the sides of the ship. He would tell the Riggers what he wanted, and where he wanted it done. The Riggers would get us set up, then stand around, and drink coffee the rest of the day. They did a lot of hollering about how slow, and stupid we were.

We had four riggers, all were Seaman from the Deck Division. Each was a suck butt of the first order. They held your Liberty Card, and if you didn't chip paint fast enough, they weren't suppose to give you Liberty that night. That would have been fine with me -- I know how to work hard. The problem was, the guys that kissed ass didn't have to work hard. They could slip one of the riggers five or ten bucks, and get early Liberty. Early Liberty was suppose to be for guys that worked real hard. I put up with this for awhile, I had a murder to get done, and I didn't want any problems.

The next two months zipped by. I was working my ass off when we were in port, learning my Flight Quarters job, when we out shaking down with the Squadron. Plus a couple nights a week, keeping track of Fine from a distance, when we were in port. I was a busy little sailor. Two weeks before leaving on West-pack, we had what the Navy calls, a Family Cruise. Moms, Dads, sisters, brothers, girls friends and plain old friends were invited aboard for a day of operations at sea.

Good was from Oklahoma and Wolf was from Mississippi, they had no one they wanted to invite, so I ask for their slots and got them. With my three slots, that gave me nine people I could invite. I could have my whole family of four, and the Chiefs' as well. T he Saratogs X.O. Wanted that ship looking good at all times, but damn, he was like a crazy man before Family Cruise. Every space on the ship, from the engine room to the bridge, had to shine inside and out. For two weeks before the cruise, officers had to attend readiness meetings in the Wardroom twice daily. When the X.O. goes crazy for cleaning, every man jack in the crew better go crazy, for cleaning as well!

The X.O. was a big believer in Moms, I know this from a dirty trick my Mother played on me about three months into our West Pack Cruise. I'll tell you now, it may give you a little insight, and maybe a laugh. Like a lot of seventeen year old boys, I wasn't a good correspondent. Mom would write, tell me everything going on at home, and ask a lot of questions about what I was doing. I wasn't thoughtful enough to take a little time and write.

The truth be known , I clearly remember thinking I'm a man mow, nobody can make me write. My dear Mother had been a World War II bride and understood the world, and the military much better than I. The letter I received, about a week before Mom lowered the boom, ended with a little P.S. You will write.

We were getting ready to pull in at one of the worlds great liberty ports, Hong Kong, and I was ready to do my drunken Sailor bit. I was under the number 1 elevator, hanging a net for side cleaners, when I hear " AIRMAN APPRENTICE AUSTIN REPORT TO THE EXCUTIVE OFFICERS CABIN." No airman apprentice gets called to the X. Os. cabin, if your Mom died they only called you to the Chaplains Office. By this time I was the Lead Rigger for Side Cleaners, so the only thing I could think was, I had fucked up cleaning the X. Os. Ship.

I had no idea where the X. Os cabin was, some where up in Officers Country. I did know I wasn't allowed in that part of the ship, in dirty dungarees. I headed for the Master at Arms Office. I told the first Class on duty, who I was and what had happened. He made a call and said, " Sailor you don't have time to get cleaned up, follow me, the X.O. wants your ass up their now." I felt sick to my stomach, just the week before Pappy Hayford had told me there was a chance he could get me to UDT training, if I kept my nose clean till the end of the cruise. At the time, I felt like my nose was anything but clean.

Pappy Hayford was standing with a Marine, in the passage way outside the X. Os cabin. The Marine was in his class "A" uniform, he opened the door and ushered Pappy and myself into a small waiting room, off the main cabin. He said "Mr Hayford, Sir, the Executive Officer said for you to come right in, I'll stay with Austin and fill him in. Pappy looked at me, pulled out a handkerchief, and started rubbing dirt off my face. He stood back, looked at me and said " Austin you are a mess." With those words of encouragement he went through the door, into the main cabin.

The Marine was Sergeant Robert Brooks, then, a by the book, white wall hair cut, spit shined shoes, sea going bell hop. Ya, that's right, today he is the FBIs Special Agent in charge of catching yours truly, Karl Austin, but more of that later. Sergeant Brooks told me that when the X.O. had me come in, I was to walk to the front of his desk, come to attention, salute, uncover (take my hat off), and remain at attention until told otherwise. Brooks said I would do well to say nothing but yes Sir, unless ask a direct question, then answer.

I was left standing, watching the clock on the wall, for 45 minutes. I wanted to leak my lizard, I w anted a smoke, I wanted to stop sweating, I wanted to be anywhere but waiting to see the X.O.! To put it mildly, I was scared shitless. I was finally called in and preformed all the rituals that confirmed I knew who was in charge. Airman Apprentice Austin, I have received a letter from your Mother, in which she asks me several questions.

My jaw must have dropped, the X. Os. next words were "close your mouth Austin, you look stupid. Sailor, you better listen up, I consider a Mother, the most important person in their children's life. A person who forsakes their Mother can stoop no lower." Mom had told the X.O. that it was my first time away from home, and she was worried if I had enough blankets, as I caught cold frequently. She was also quite concerned about the people I hung around with, as I could be easily led down the wrong path. Was I attending church services regularly? She was worried, as she had not heard from me since the ship had left Lone Beach.

"Now Austin, Mr. Hayford tells me your Mother was on our Family Cruise, and that she is a delightful woman. She is obviously also a woman who gets what she wants, read this little note she inserted in her letter to me."

He handed me one of those three by five cards my Mom used for recipes. She had written: "You have my permission to place my letter to YOU, On a bulletin board, so the crew may read it." My Mothers' signature was on the bottom. Good God, she had dropped the big one on me from halfway around the world! The X.O. asked me if I was going to write my Mother, YES Sir. He said he though two letters a month sounded about right to him, did I agree? Yes Sir. " See that the first letter is on Mr. Hayford desk before you go on liberty again." Yes Sir. "Do not let your Mother down again Austin." No Sir. Dismissed, I was out of their as fast my knocking knees could carry my young ass. The X.O. was right, Mothers are a big deal, mine had just reached half way around the world, grabbed my ear, and guided me.

THE TERRORIST

Our Family Cruise went off without a hitch, for me and the ship. The X.O. had done us all proud, even the guys with no loved ones on board got into it. The ship and crew shined that day. One thing I found strange was language, I didn't hear one swear word all day. It was like some swear switch had been shut off in every crew member's head. Most women did not know how bad the language got, when there were no women around.

I had covertly recorded six young guys, my self included, just setting around playing cards and shooting the breeze. After thirty minutes, I let the rest of the guys know that we had been recorded, and played tile tape back. It was strange, we ad been swearing so much, we couldn't understand what we had been talking about. Just another strange thing that got stuck in my mind, something for my little brain cells to worry over. Human inconsistency and self-control. It would all come together for me one sick, sad, drunken mourning far down the chain of my life.

Boats rode on my back or sat on my lap all day. My dad, the Chief and J.D. were nonstop, all over the skip, we only saw them at demonstrations. Mom and the Chiefs wife Judy had every guy in the division, whose Mom wasn't there, adopted for the day. My brother's Jim and Steve, the Chiefs girls, Patty, Susan and Judith Jo were like their own little family. What was funny, Judith Jo the youngest was acting the part of the Mother with Jim as Dad. She was in charge and they all happily followed her.

I remember setting with Boats, in some chairs they had setup in Hanger Bay #one, just setting and watching. Dad, Chief and J.D. rode the elevator down to the hanger with a couple planes from the flight deck. Boats and I sat there and watched the three of them move around the hanger, looking at different displays and talking. They were an odd looking threesome. I had never payed any attention to how small J.D. was, Dad was about six feet, Chief a couple inches taller, J.Ds. head only came to my Dads shoulder.

As they moved around they were looking up and down at each other as they took turns talking, J.D. would disappear from view behind one or the other of them. The only way you could tell he was still there, Dad and Chief would be looking down. You could watch these three men, never hear a word they said, and tell they not only liked but respected each other.

The question of why I had been such an asshole toward my own Father shouted in my brain, the thought was like a big noise rolling around in my head. Years later I would understand, at the time I could only hug Boats and tell him, be good to your Dad.

Sailors are always bitching about the food, telling anyone that might give them some sympathy, like mothers, how bad the food is. The truth is, the chow is pretty damn good most of the time, maybe not Mom standard, but not bad at all. Our Navy cooks made liars of every sailor who had bitched, on Family Cruise day. I mean first class, top of the line, melt in your mouth

Mom food. I heard more then one Mother say something like, Bobby, I thought you said the food was disgusting, you should be ashamed, this food is excellent. I heard a Mother tell one of the cooks, she was sorry that her son did not appreciate the hard work they did turning out such fine meals!

The Family Cruise in some strange way was the cap to all our shake down cruises, we were battle ready. On all are shake downs something had not been done right, one damn thing or another had not lived up to our Captains expectations. With Moms looking on, as we went through all our drills, no one wanted to look bad. I guess we were all like the cooks, a little extra effort for our loved ones, who's Mom would accept less.

As the ship pulled back into Long Beach, everyone not required to run the ship, and all our guests gathered on the flight deck. The Captain made a speech thanking everyone, loved ones and crew, alike. The last few words of that speech have stuck in mind for all these years: "It is my daily payer that we are always ready to use the awesome power you have seen on display today, and with Gods grace, it is never necessary. Thank you. "

The Chief, invited me down to San Diego, the weekend before we where to leave for West Pack. Judy and the kids would be in Arkansas visiting with her family. Chief said he knew a First Class Petty Officer in UDT 11 that would show us around their area, over on the Anphib Base, in Coronado. I told Chief, if I was given liberty, I would be there, with bells on, head to toe.

Time was closing in on Fine, I had to get him, sometime in the next two weeks. We would leave for West Pack the Wednesday after my visit with the Chief, I wanted it done with before that weekend. The ship was in port from the end of the Family Cruise, until our departure for West Pack. Being on Side Cleaners, I had what was called Watch Standers Liberty. Kind of a misnomer, as Side Cleaners normally stood no watches, if you kept the ship clean you had liberty every night the ship was in port.

My murder of First Class Petty Officer Gary Fine went down just as planed. The problems came from three things after the murder, that I hadn't figured correctly. Number one was my reaction, after all I had killed those two child molesters at the market, and it still didn't bother me, not in the least. Number two, I didn't think it would make the news in San Diego. Number three, I thought I waited long enough after Fine kicked my ass to murder him. I hadn't, my name came up. I needed a lot of luck to get away with it.

I killed him Friday night before going to San Diego. I had called the Chief and told him I was going to get some Surfing in Friday evening, early Saturday mourning, at the Trestles near Camp Pendleton, and would be at his house by ten in the morning on Saturday.

I don't know why Fine never brought a woman home

with him at night. In the over two months I'd been sneaking and peeking around behind Fine, he only saw other guys' wives during the day. If they stayed the night at his place, they didn't go out. I guess he was just one of those guys that liked sneaky sex. I knew that if I was laying up on that landing and he brought a woman home with him, I was not going to kill her too. If that happened, I was going to drop off the back side of the landing as they came up the stairs, and run my ass off.

Fine didn't go out till Friday. All week I had a rising fear that I might have waited too long. Friday night everything went my way. I laid up on that landing, in the dark, for a little over two hours. When Fine staggered up the stairs he caught one round in the forehead, he went straight down, just crumpled in tile middle of the stairs. I was on automatic. This murder had been gone over in my mind so many times, I could have done it in my sleep.

As soon as the hammer fell, I knew I had done wrong. I also knew I couldn't stop and think now. Get moving , follow the plan. My mind was not working right. If anything had not gone as planned, I wouldn't have gotten away.

When I could finally let myself think, it was around four in the morning, and I was sitting on my surfboard 300 hundred yards off the beach we called Trestles, at Camp Pendleton, about halfway to San Diego. All I could do was sit on my board and cry.

I had been taught all my life murder was wrong, but it was clear in my mind that the one all powerful God was letting me know there was a big difference between what I had just done, and my first two kills. I sat there just wanting to undo what I had done. Knowing man might make me pay the same price for all my murders, but God would make me suffer for the last one and let me slide on the first two.

Around six thirty I was still sitting there shaking cold. I hadn't taken off on one wave and the long shore current had taken me a couple miles down the coast. I took the first wave in and headed for my wagon. I had to talk to the Chief.

When I got to the house, it was just the Chief and me. Judy and the kids were in Arkansas. I had tried to get a hold of myself on the drive down, but I wasn't in their home five minutes when the Chief ask me what the problem was? Everything but me seemed to be in slow motion. I mumbled some bullshit and spilled the coffee Chief had poured me. He laughed and told me to get a hold of myself. I didn't want to look stupid when we went to the UDT area. Just being around him calmed me down.

We drank a couple cups of coffee, read the paper, talked about the new nuclear ships the navy was building, and somehow, what I had done was no longer in charge, it was tucked away. Not gone, never gone, just tucked away.

THE TERRORIST

We took the ferry to Coronado and drove over to the Naval Amphibious Base. I was finally going to meet real, live Navy Frogmen, and see their training area. For me, what and where I most wanted to be.

The town of Coronado was on the tip of a long spit of land that formed the west side of San Diego Harbor. The town itself was between the Naval Air Station and the Amphibian Base, a beautiful little town looking across the harbor entrance toward San Diego. I hoped one day this place would be my home.

The Chief and I went to the UDT Training Area to meet his friend, a First Class Petty Officer by the name of Vince Alovaira. There was no training class in progress, just a collection of old, very stark World War II buildings. I hung on every word out of Alovaira mouth. My eyes his watched every move he made. He was the real thing. The hardest of the hard.

It's not Underwater Demolition Teams anymore, it's now SEAL TEAM. The old stark buildings have been replaced. But that first four months of training is still what Vince told me that day: Four months of nothing but physical and mental HARASSMENT, you can leave anytime you want, they will cut you a set of orders to some nice duty station in a heartbeat. Vince took us over to the obstacle course, showed us around the area and generally seemed like a nice guy. That is till he looked me in the eye and said "My job is to make sure no pussies make it through training."

He said it in a way that made you believe as long as he was there, no pussies would pass. Standing on the upstream side of training, I had no idea what it meant to put everything -- and I do mean every fiber of your body and soul -- out there to become a Navy Frogman. As we were leaving, Vince gave me a little smile and told me, "It is easy to get through training, just don't break any bones and never quit." He spoke the pure truth, but until I was on the downstream side of training, and had the luck not to break any parts of my body, all my thoughts were pure bullshit.

The Chief and I drove on down to Mexico and spent a little time wandering around Tijuana sucking down a few good Mexican beers and watching all the drunk Sailors and Marines drinking, fighting and whoring. I would have been right in there with the rest of the animals as I still had no idea what the word moderation meant, but I was with the Chief and he did not go for that kind of shit.

We drove back to his home, me running my mouth a mile a minute, Chief just making little comments that kept my jaw flapping. He told me "I do enjoy that strange mind of yours Karl, you have an odd way of seeing life. You're either smart or full of shit, I'm not sure which."

I had a hard time going to sleep when we got home. Fine was with me. I couldn't talk with anyone about what I had done, just run the thoughts around in my mind. I know it was after four in the mourning before I dropped into a troubled sleep.

When I woke, the sun was coming in through the living room window and the sheets where no longer on the couch but on the floor. When I turned my head to the side, there sat the Chief, in a big chair, just staring at me with all three eyeballs. The Sunday papers were lying at his feet. He did not say a word or take his eyes of me. He reached down and picked up a part of the paper. When he turned the paper toward me, Chief had his big finger on a small picture. I couldn't see it, but I knew it was Fine.

He said, "Karl do not say a word. If anyone asks, you got here just after eleven o'clock Friday night, you went surfing around five in the morning. Tell the rest of the weekend as it happened. If you don't stick to that story, I'll rip off your head and shit down your neck! Get up now, go home and see your Mother." He got up and walked out of the room.

After I left the house, I stopped and picked up the Sunday papers. On the front page of the local section, was a small picture of Fine, and a three-column article that ended on the back page. He had grown up in San Diego, they gave a little history of his life and told as much as was known about the murder -- not much.

Like most stories in the paper it was not much more then circle talk, but it had been dumb of me to assume they wouldn't hear of the murder in San Diego. Not only shouldn't I have murdered Fine but when I did, I made a crap job of it.

I was in a forced calm for the next four days. Mom was the only one to notice that I wasn't my normal hyper self. She chalked it up to me being nervous about leaving my family, and the good old U.S.A. for seven months. I went home for dinner with my family every night, until the ship left for Westpac Wednesday afternoon. Fine's murder had, of course, made the local papers. He had surely told someone about kicking my ass -- Chief had figured it out -- who else would?

When the Saratoga pulled away from the pier in Long Beach, heading out on our seven-month cruise, there was no sailor on board that ship as relived to be underway as me. My relief was definitely premature.

Less then twenty-four hours out of Long Beach, Pappy Hayford had me come down to the Division office. He told me that the legal officer wanted to talk with me, in the Master at Arms office and asked if I new what it was about.

No Sir. Pappy asked if I would like him to go with me? Yes Sir. Thank God for Pappy, most Division Officers would have said nothing. It gave me a little time to get myself together. I knew damn well what it was about. Fine.

When we got to the Master at Arms office, Pappy asked the Legal Officer if he could give him a few minutes before he talked with me. Of course he got it, which gave me another twenty minutes, standing outside the office, getting my lies and truths in the correct order. It seemed the Inglewood Police wanted to interview me, about the murder of Petty Officer First Class Gary Fine, and my whereabouts last Friday night.

Pappy was sitting right there when I told the Legal Officer where I was Friday night. About Fine's lies when he enlisted me in the Navy, and the ass whipping he gave me at the pizza place that night. I told the Legal Officer that I hadn't done anything wrong, and I did not want to miss the cruise, just to tell the police the same thing I had told him. He didn't seem to know what was going to happen, I was dismissed and told to stand by in the Division coffee locker.

Pappy walked out with me and said "Don't worry Austin, I'm sure the Executive Officer will do the right thing. I'll let you know soon."I! t took more then two hours, I must have had six or seven cups of coffee -- you might say I was a nervous wreck.

J.D. was in the coffee locker trying to do his paper work. He finally got tired of me pacing back and forth. J.D. told me to sit, shut up, and deal the Crib game. God bless old J.D., he played Cribbage with me for the better part of two hours. He told me that if I had been at the Chief's house Friday night, I had nothing to worry about. The X.O. would never fly me back. I might have to make a sworn statement or something, but that would be about it.

One thing that was funny, Wolf and his running mate Good, couldn't figure out why, I was sitting in the coffee locker playing cards with J.D., when it was still working hours. They kept poking their heads in the hatch, with that, what the hell is going on look, on their faces. J.D. kept a blank look on his face. He would ask them questions about the work on our fuel system, nod his head and tell them, "sounds good, get back to it."

They were driving themselves nuts trying to figure out why I didn't have to work. When Pappy finally came to the coffee locker the whole damn Division was there taking a break. He caused quite a stir when he asked me to step out on the catwalk for a minute. Now everyone got that, what the hell is going on look, on their faces.

J.D. had been close to right: They had checked my alibi by radio/phone patch and the Chief had backed me up. They then called the Inglewood Police, told them I had been interviewed, and they were satisfied that I was in San Diego at the time in question.

The X.O. would not fly me back at this time, but would forward my notarized statement to them, and make me available for a further interview, aboard the ship, when we reached Pearl Harbor Hawaii. God bless the Chief. When we pulled into Pearl Harbor and no cops showed up, I was home free. At least the cops didn't seem to be interested in me any longer.

Somehow the strange twins, Good and Wolf knew I did

it. They didn't care how many times I said no it wasn't me. One would look a the other and say something like, “I think our good buddy Karl is a murderer” The other would shake his head up and down, and say “I wonder if he will give us a cut-rate when we want someone done in.”

One night after we secured from Flight Quarters, the three of us were having a smoke in the catwalk. It was three or four in the mourning and we where whipped -- just standing under God’s beautiful night sky, trying to come down after hours of screaming Jets. No one had said anything for a while when Good popped out with "Karl we like you a lot, maybe because you are stranger then us. We won't talk about you killing that guy anymore.” With that they both walked off.

I'm not going to tell you my whole life, not even most of it , some good, some bad and how I feel about it, that's what you get. Here is the sex part, I like strong women, like the song says " WHEN YOU’RE HOT, YOU’RE HOT, WHEN YOU’RE NOT, YOU’RE NOT " and sex can be beautiful or ugly but it’s always DANGEROUS. Be careful.

After I murdered Fine, the question I most had to answer for myself was, what laws count and how do you sort man’s law from God’s? Well like most of you who care, I’m still struggling with the question. The easiest part to figure out was telling the difference between God’s and man’s laws that effect us in this life.

I'll give you the first example that became clear to me. People all over the world, no matter their race, no matter their culture, whether they come from highlands or from savannas, every damn one of us walks the same or we don't walk. God's law of gravity is equal for all, dumb, smart, rich, poor. If you don't do it right you fall down. Any law that is not equal for all, is man's law. I keep it simple, I may not understand God's law for this life, but I find no problem in separating it from man's.

The Recruiting Poster said " JOIN THE NAVY AND SEE THE WORLD ", it should add, through the swinging doors of a bar. Every port we hit had an area of bar, after bar that catered to our search for the perfect drunk. My problems with alcohol would not have lasted as long as they did, if my capacity had not been so large, and the effect so odd. It effected me like some SUPER SPEED, I wouldn't pass out and I didn't stumble much. Of course, for me, moderation never entered the picture. I never wanted too just sip a few. Slam it back and get more, was my mode of operation.

Another big problem for me and those around me, when I drank, the teeny amount of inhibition that kept me close to the lower bounds of what is excepted in our society, totally disappeared. I won't bore you with details of all my drunken visits to foreign lands but for those who never served, and to give you some insight into my young mind, I'll fill you in on the first and last drunk of that cruise.

Our first liberty port after Pearl Harbor, was Subic Bay

THE TERRORIST

Philippines. More bars and whores per square inch then any place I've ever been. They were everywhere -- upstairs, downstairs, around back, across the street. There was no pretense at tourism -- it was pure knee wobbling . . . gutter crawling . . . drunken lust.

For a young man raised in the Fifties, Subic Bay, known far and wide as Pubic Bay, was a big dose of culture shock. The girls ranged in age from thirteen to around twenty. They were earning money to support their families and most of them where proud of it. My young seventeen-year-old self was in culture shock, going from Bar to Bar, having a drink, checking out the bar girls and moving to the next. I was in hog heaven, the bars were packed with Sailors and Marines all jostling for room at the bar or competing for the best looking whore.

These girls where tough, and lived by a code, all their own. Most of them carried, and knew how to use six or seven inch Flip knives. When closed the blade is between the two hinged half's of the handle. A flip of the wrist and the blade was in the ready to use position. They called them Butterfly Knives, untrue lovers where called Butterflies, it was no coincidence.

I walked into a bar just off the main drag, down by the market square, a huge place called The Anchors Away. The place had a live band, a big dance floor and a large game room off the back. I got a beer, and wandered toward a raised area with tables off the right side of the bandstand. In the back of the raised area stood Whilly, Hartso and their running mate Pinkoff, a huge fat First

Class cook. Everyone on the ship said, "Don't mess around with those guys, they're bad dudes and enjoy hurting people." Well I worked for two of them, they treated me pretty good, and I sure wasn't going to cross them.

The three of them and a bunch off Sailors and Marines were standing around a table looking down toward two guys sitting across from each other. When I got close enough to see what was going on, one of the guys was the kiss-ass rigger from side cleaners. The other was some Sailor I didn't know. They sat facing each other, each with one forearm laying on the table, pressed up against the other guy's forearm. There was a lit cigarette laying in the grove, between their forearms, smoke curling up, the smell of burning flesh in the air.

Whilly had a beer in one hand and a fist full of money in the other -- he was the only one not cheering them on. He just stood there holding the bet money and sipping his beer. Now this particular rigger was what I call a worm. He didn't hang any nets or stages, which was his job, but worse, he was one of the guys selling early liberty.

The game was called BURN, the first guy to move his arm lost. It is a dumb game and only dumb people play it. I freely admit that at that stage of my life I was DUMB a good part of the time. I watched the worm win twice.

Whilly looked at me and said "tough little fucker." I

didn't even think. My mouth just opened and said, "I can beat him." Whilly said here's twenty bucks, says you can't. Well I only had twelve dollars, enough money on a good drunk in those days. The guy who had just lost said he would cover the rest.

If you have seen any of the pictures they have shown around of me at that age, you know I didn't cut an imposing figure. I was six foot one inch and one hundred sixty-five pounds, with the face of a young fourteen-year-old. I didn't scare people with my massive frame and hard countenance. What I had was a no quit mentality, even when I had let my hippo mouth overload my hamster ass.

It only took about ten minutes and I had him. I hadn't even looked at the worm. He had taken a just lit Lucky Strike out of his mouth, gave me a little smirk and dropped it in the crease between our forearms. I had sat and bullshitted with anyone that wanted to talk. I had one of the bar girls get me a beer. When the worm tried to talk to me I just ignored him.

About the time our burning skin was over shadowing the bar stink, I looked at him, winked, and blew him a little kiss. He lost it. The worm jumped up and started calling me names. I couldn't help it -- the more he yelled, the harder I laughed. Whilly was calling the worm a stupid fucker, telling him he had let me psyche him out. The worm wanted another chance, double or nothing. Whilly wouldn't bet on him. He said "You want to lose money you stupid fucker, lose your own."

The worm put up his own twenty, I covered it with my new winnings and we went at it again. This time I locked eyes with him and never said a word. He didn't last five minutes this time. When he pulled away, he got up and just kept walking. I had two burns on my forearm and forty-four dollars in my pocket. Pinkoff bought me a beer. Whilly said you stick with us. Hartso didn't care about anything -- he had a young lady setting on his lap, and one feeding him beer.

After about an hour, things were getting a little fuzzy. Whilly, Hartso and Pinkoff were standing by the edge of the raised area, their big bodies close, their heads right together talking over the band. Pinkoff kept pointing to the far end of the bar, where seven or eight Marines were minding their own business, knocking back booze. He was pretty damn agitated, and looked funny, his big fat body jiggling every time he gestured with his arms. I kept thinking about the Pillsbury Dough Boy -- that is, till he turned and pointed to me. He had sweat running down his big face, and didn't look funny anymore. Whilly gestured for me to come over. Of course I went. As I reached them, he and Pinkoff put their big arms over my shoulders, I felt very small.

They wanted me to go over to the Marines, and call them Candy Asses then just head back across the dance floor and get out of the way. Whilly said the three of them were going to kick those Marines' asses. He said for me to get myself over by the door, as we would be getting the hell out of there fast when they were done. I was well past the point of having any inhibition or sense and was fortified with large amounts of courage in a bottle. So of course I said "No Problem."

I stood about ten feet from the Marines and screamed at the top of my lungs, "Hey you Candy Ass Marines." When they turned to see who the idiot was, I pointed back across the dance floor and screamed: "Those guys are going to kick your asses." As I headed back across the dance floor, several of the Marines were following me . I walked right past the mean and nasty triplets, went to our table, picked up my beer and turned around.

The fight was on, some poor guy had just hit Pinkoff. It had no affect on him at all. He grabbed the poor sucker, slammed him into a pole, and leaned his huge gut onto the guy, to hold him in place. Both of Pinkoff's hands were free, doubled into great ham fists. His arms were moving back and forth slamming his fist into the poor guys ribs. Pinkoff just held him there with his weight and beat the shit out of him. Another Marine was standing at Pinkoff's side, smacking him in the head. Pinkoff paid no attention.

The whole damn place turned into complete chaos -- some guys were joining in, some where heading for the doors. I headed for the doors. Outside was almost as crazy, some drunk Sailor took a swing at me, one of those wide looping out of control things. A short little punch to his face, and he was on his ass. When the three of them came out the door, Hartso was throwing anyone he could get his hands on. Whilly had some poor Marine's head stuck under his arm, and was dragging him along as he hit him in the face. Pinkoff was covered in blood, his and others peoples. We walked around to the other side of the square and up the street to another Bar. From that day on, I was a made man on the USS Saratoga. Dumb-huh!

With in a week of that drunken liberty, Whilly made me a Rigger. It ticked off the other riggers, as they were all Seaman from First Division, and I was breaking in on their racket. They got madder as time wore on, I was giving early liberty to the hardest workers in my crew and doing my own rigging. My crew got more work done, which didn't endear me with the other riggers. But then I had never been what you might call popular. Two weeks after making rigger, Whilly made me Lead Seaman of Side Cleaning Gang, this caused a lot of hard feelings.

Whilly handled it in his usual way. Four riggers told Hartso they wouldn't work for me. When Whilly heard about it, he called the four riggers and me down to the Bow Chain Locker. Whilly asked the other riggers if they had told me they wouldn't work for me, none of them had. He then asked if any of them would like to try to whip his ass, no one said anything. Whilly said, " Whip my ass or work for who I say, now you four get the fuck back to work ." They hauled ass out of there. " Austin you better find that big one alone and kick his ass good, put an end to it."

The big one's name was Jimmy Pole. He liked to run his

jaw and work himself up to a fight, so I just walked up and hit him as hard as I could. He got nailed three times and went down. I hit him once more when he tried to get up! Jimmy Pole and the three other riggers did their job and steered clear of me.

I have never liked fighting but there are things in this life worth fighting for. At times nothing will improve the situation but an old fashioned, down in the dirt, fist fight. If you will not stand and fight for what is yours, someone will take it. The truth is you don't even have to win. If you will fight most people know it and will leave you alone. Keep in mind all violence is not bad, ask any woman who has killed someone that was trying to hurt her children. I don't understand mans law's about violence, they're stupid. God's are a lot clearer for me.

Hong Kong has always amazed me. If it can't be bought in Hong Kong, it can't be bought any where in the world. It is a rugged mountain of humanity that shoots up out of the sea, just off the coast of mainland China. It is one of the places in this world you could transport me to in my sleep and I would know where I was before I woke. Hong Kong has its own taste, smell and feel. I love the place.

My first time in Hong Kong I did nothing but walk and look, the place just overwhelmed me. People lived on the roofs of buildings, in holes in walls going up stairs. Whole families lived and worked in little shops. The harbor was full of boats of every description and the boats were full of people. Everyone was doing some kind of work. I spent one day watching these Chinese working on building a high-rise The scaffolding was twenty-four stories of tied together Bamboo with little rickety Bamboo ladders to climb. These guys carried or pulled everything up that scaffolding by hand and back. They were WORKERS! I mean they stood head and shoulders above any workers I had ever seen.

I had been standing on the street across from the construction site, when a Chinaman with a push cart started up the hill toward me. What ever it was under the blanket on that cart was heavy because he and the two small children with him would push a few feet, stop chock the wheels of the cart, gather their strength and do it again. It was a long steep hill, they had set a pace and paid no attention to the cars, bikes, rickshaws and humanity that speed past them.

I don't know why, maybe I just wanted the cart up the hill, but I walked down there and started pushing when they did. Good God did this cause a stir! The Chinese on the street all stopped and were looking and pointing at me. When we chocked the cart, we had gotten halfway up the hill What had stopped us was people slowing down, some stopping to look. We couldn't go any further. There was a lot of conversation going on that I couldn't understand, but it was obvious it had to do with me pushing the cart.

Damn, the next thing I knew, <u>all</u> traffic was stopped. Two cops worked their way to the cart and started asking questions. Thank God one of them was asking me questions in the King's English. I told him what had happened when I started to help pushing the cart. Those two cops took charge. They got everyone moving in front of the cart. Two other Chinese helped us push the cart into an alley near the top of the hill.

The Chinese Policeman was nice, but explained that anything that impeded the free flow of traffic in Hong Kong was taken very seriously. The cart owner could lose his license, and I could be fined for what had just happened. Please do not do this again. He went on to explain that it may be no problem for me to pay a fine, but if this family lost their cart license they could not deliver their Carved furniture. My mouth must of been hanging open, my mind was screaming, I just wanted to help. Everyone was speaking in Chinese again and the guy with the cart was looking at me and bowing as he spoke.

The cop told me the guy with cart's name was Wong and he thanked me for my help and was sorry to bring so much trouble on me. Hell, they were doing fine, until I stuck my nose in. I asked the cop to beg their forgiveness as it was me who caused all the problems. For some reason as the cop passed on what I had said, I bowed. Everyone was bowing all around with smiles even the cops. The cop said he knew this family and they were exceptional carvers. If I would like, he would ask if I might see what they was on the cart.

The truth was I had no interest, but to be polite I said yes please. When the pad came off I became interested. It was beautiful. The cart held a chest, made from some dark wood, about two feet, by two feet, by six feet long. It was covered in carving, deep and perfectly formed. It depicted a village, people and all. Beautiful, beautiful was all I could say. The whole top was a birds-eye vies, like looking down from a forty-five degree angle, little houses, people, roads, trees, hills and even a water well.

I was invited to come to their shop the next day. Wong would meet me at Fenwick Pier, where the Liberty Launches landed, around noon. Everyone bowed and shook hands, the cart was behind the store where the chest was to be delivered. No one lost a license, or was fined and the police even seemed pleased.

As I rode the Liberty Launch back to the Saratoga, I wondered why me helping push a cart had caused such a stir? I knew It was because I wasn't Chinese, but why did most of the Whites, Colored and Filipinos on the ship stay in their own little group? Why in the Hell did I never stay in one little group? I couldn't say why, I just figured I was right and most of you were screwed up.

J. D. explained a few facts of life to me that night, when I told him about the invitation. He said these people were poorer then I could understand, and our cultures were so different that I could screw up, just talking to the wrong person first. He said to me, “If Wong doesn't speak English, and you don’t speak Chinese, how in the Hell are you going to communicate, call a cop?”

J. D. went to his locker, and got a English to Chinese Dictionary, he handed it to me and said, "Good Luck. Make sure you take some food as a gift. They will most likely feed you, and can ill afford it. Karl the best advice I can give you, is be polite, and hope for the best." There it was again. J. D. seemed to think me being a guest at the carving shop, was odd, and might be a problem. Why is the Human Race like this?

Wong was at the landing when I got of the Liberty Launch. He greeted me with a clear Hello. I would find out his English was better then I thought. I had used J. D. dictionary to find the words..... <u>First market please</u>. I'm sure my context was wrong, but Wong figured out what I wanted. We took a rickshaw to a large open air market.

I had my plan all worked out. I just went around bowing, and saying "English please." In short order, an old Chinese lady asked if she could help. I told her where I was going, and asked her to help me pick out the right food as a gift. The old lady seemed to take my request seriously, she spoke with Wong, in Chinese for a couple minutes, shaking her head up and down. She told me this is a traditional family. I should take a duck -- do not take two, that would be to much. I should give the duck to Wong's Grandmother. With that we walked down the street to buy a duck.

I loved the smell of that Market. There was more strange food on display then I had ever seen. Live food, dried food, and every damn food in between. She checked each duck out, God knows for what, but she made me feel I was in the hands of the world's greatest duck expert.

Wong, our newly purchased duck, and I walked to the carving shop, about a quarter mile from the market. The shop was part of a big old warehouse, that had been partitioned off into what seemed like hundreds of sections. Each space contained people working and living. The spaces varied in size and construction. Most where quite small, many with nothing more then canvas walls. There where a few large spaces with wooden walls, the large ones all had second stories.

People where everywhere, going about the business of living in a way I had never imagined. The smell, taste and feel of Hong Kong comes from those millions of people, living one on top of another, in every space available. The carving shop was one of the larger spaces in the warehouse, and took up two floors. They built the tables, chest, armoires, and such on the top floor and they did the carving and finishing on the bottom floor.

They could pick up part of the floor and lower large pieces, with a block and tackle, from the second floor to the first. One wall of the bottom floor had a large set of doors that opened on to an aisle in the warehouse. This family was rich, not by any standard most Americans would understand, but in the world of the warehouse they were at the top of the heap.

I had no intent to disrupt this family, but it was even apparent to even my teenage brain, that I was being treated as an honored quest or a long lost relative. Wong presented me to his family, grandparents first. As I presented Grandmother with the Duck, I was thinking, Wong's English may be accented, but it gets better by the second.

He later apologized and explained -- it was always better to let the police know as little about you as possible. Made sense to me. He was sorry for not helping me at the market, I had surprised him with my bowing and saying, English please. I had probably embarrassed him with my lack of inhibition --the Chinese are publicly very restrained. Wong introduced me to all fourteen members of his family.

Every member of the family was involved in the making , carving, sales and delivery of the furniture. Wong's father seemed to be the head builder and carver, but Grandfather was in charge of everything. I was given a walk through tour of the building and carving process. There were several large pieces in different stages of completion. The tour ended behind a canvas partition, near the big doors on the first floor.

Every piece I saw was beautiful, but what was behind the canvas was unlike anything I have ever seen. A large armoire with double doors, every inch carved, but in a way that it appeared the whole thing had grown that way. The carving told the story of Hong Kong, under the rule of Great Britain. It had been commissioned as a gift for Queen Elizabeth's Birthday.

The piece had been commissioned by a refugee group to honor the Queen. Most of the people stacked one on top of another on this small Island, had escaped from Communist China . These people lived like shit, but were happy to be in Hong Kong. What must their life have been like in China, if this was better? Wong and his family had escaped on a Junk, and sailed about three hundred miles down the coast of China to Hong Kong. They dodged the Chinese Communists all the way.

They had lived and started their carving business on the Junk for the first year and half. Three of them, his Grandfather, Father and Wong had been exclusively involved in building and carving objects for sale. The rest had gotten any job they could, to bring in money. They worked on the carving when they weren't at another job. After a year and a half, they had earned enough money to sell the Junk and lease the two story shop in the warehouse.

As I walked back to the landing that night, through the swarming mass of Chinese, I new the true blessings of the United States of America. Wong and his family had given me a gift, thankfulness. It was real clear to me, the only Prayer I needed was, Thank you Lord.

I'm not telling you this because I'm proud of it, but of all the liberties on that seven month cruise, that's the only one I wasn't just a drunken, women chasing, bar room fighting sailor. It's the one that still gives me things to smile, and think about to this day.

Pappy Hayford had let me know there was a chance I could go to UDT Training at the end of this cruise. That meant I had to be ready, big IF, if I got the chance. Each candidate had to submit a request chit, and have it approved up the chain of command. You had to do an interview, then take a run, swim and P.T. test. The swimming would be no sweat, that was in the bag. What I was worried about was the running.

I had never done any serious running. The morning after pulling out of Hong Kong I started running on the flight deck, when there were no flight operations. I ran about five miles that first morning, up and down the flight deck. Wind to my face, wind to my back, it was a pleasant morning. Only Sergeant Brooks, and another Marine, were on the flight deck doing a P.T. routine. Each time I passed, they were doing a different exercise. Maybe Brooks would help me with a work-out routine?

After my first run I knew pain! My upper legs and shins were killing me, every step I took hurt. It shocked me, that the little bit of running I had done, caused me so much pain. Oh well, Wolf and Good led the harassment. Guys, even friends, always pounce when they find a weakness.

I didn't quit, but for the next two weeks I only ran – let's say limped -- two miles everyday. One night after flight operations, Sergeant Brooks was up on the flight deck, when I finished limping my two miles. My legs still hurt, I had run everyday for two weeks, and things were not getting better.

I approached Brooks, and explained the problem I was having. Brooks did this silly shit all the time, maybe he could tell me why it wasn't getting easier. God Bless that Marine, he told me, " First, don't run for three days. If you want to get in shape you can run and P.T. with me, but if you're a quitter don't bother. I don' t deal with quitters."

Those three days with no running got rid of the pain. Sergeant Brooks taught me some stretch exercises, he set up a chart that required me to do varied distances on my runs. One run might be three miles, the next day he may of had me doing wind-sprints, run a hundred yards as fast as you can, do twenty-five push-ups and twenty five set-ups, ten do that all over again ten times. Sergeant Brooks' P.T. routine was one hour long, and had fifteen different exercises in it. There were over five hundred push-ups and set-ups alone. He ask me if I was going to try out for U. D .T. Training, when I answered affirmative, he said when I could do his routine we would talk about what it would take to make it through Training.

Brooks was the only Black, in those days Negro or Colored, guy I had ever spent any length of time with, but you didn't get to know him on a personal level. You got to know a one hundred present Marine. I never called him anything but Sergeant Brooks, most of you have seen him, he's the guy that is really in charge of catching my ass. You know how he comes across as the perfect FBI Agent, well that's how he was when he was a Marine, the perfect Marine. We were together part of every day for damn near six months, he is the most private person I have ever meet. I don't mean withdrawn, I mean everything that came out of him, was by the Book Marine Corps.

In the early 60s the division of the Races was a completely different thing than it is today. Most white people were not, what you would call Racist, they just figured that's how it was and couldn't be bothered to do anything about it. The funny thing was even the hard core racist stayed clear of Sergeant Brooks. They made remarks and hassled the ten or eleven coloreds guys that weren't Stewards, most everyone else let them get away with it. But none of them ever fucked with Sergeant Brooks.

I never heard or saw anyone treat Brooks with other then respect to his face, and only once did I hear something said behind his back. One night at a bar in Japan, one of the guys that worked for me on Side Cleaners, ask why I worked out with that NIGGER Marine? I told him, I'll make you a deal, if you will go call Sergeant Brooks a NIGGER to his face, I'LL tell you why I work out with him. The guy gave me a stupid look, like he didn't know what my problem was and said FUCK YOU Austin, picked up his beer and left the table.

Brooks will eat steel to get his job done. Right now I'm

his job, and I'm betting that they don't catch me. I bet I'll finish this autobiography and turn myself in. I'm the needle in a two hundred and sixty million person haystack, and I put damn near ten years planing and preparation before I shut down Los Angles . Catch me if you can, I like competing against the best and and Agent Brooks is the best.

I was a busy camper, between Flight Quarters, keeping the sides of our ship clean and being wiped into shape by Sergeant Brooks, I had no time to become bored. I was writing to Mom, that kept her happy and the XO off my ass. Judith Jo sent me such neat serious letters: What was going on in the Boats life, her mom and dad and even a few little things about herself, I had to write to her.

It was halfway through the cruise when I did Brooks' P.T. Routine, he gave me a BIG AT-A-BOY and the promised advice on what I needed to do to get through Training and into the Teams. Brooks kept it simple: He said I would never make it by myself, it is set up to break any individual. The Training is set up in a way that only Team players make it. Always carry your share, extra when you can. The guys that don't carry their share will be gone quick, the rest of you will make sure. Be in the best shape you can when you start training.

They will tear you down anyway, but being in good shape and luck will help keep you free of serious injury. He was right on the money, every word, but like many things, UDT Training moved well past words and thoughts. For me, it became the most important link in my chain of life.

The Flight Deck during operations is a an adrenaline pump, a total assault on all the senses. In those days A 3 Ds, Corsairs, Phantom and Vigilante were the monsters of the flight deck. Just walk in the wrong place, they could suck you up and spit you out in less time then it takes your heart to beat. There was jet fuel, bombs and ammunition on the flight deck as jets both took off and landed.

The guys flying these huge hunks of metal were young Naval and Marine Officers, they were the most arrogant group of humans I have ever met. They had to be arrogant, they had to believe they were God's chosen. Landing a jet that weighs thousands of pounds, on the deck of a ship that is bouncing all over the damn place is not for people of weak will.

Early one morning I was secured from flight quarters early. As usual I was wound up and needed some time to come down before I could go to sleep. They still had three Vigilantes, the biggest and the badest, to bring back before everyone was secured from Flight Quarters. I had gone up to Vulture's row, a catwalk that over looked the flight deck on the side of the Superstructure, near the bridge. Crew that were not involved in flight quarters were allowed to watch from there. I had a camera, to catch a picture of one of these huge jets hitting the deck.

The stern end of the flight deck was called the Round Down: it had no sharp edge, but was rounded off. Just past that, the Arresting Gear started, it was made up of four, inch and one half cables. Each cable stretched across the flight deck, going over a large pulley on each side, through a steel pipe to the hydraulics under the flight deck. Each jet had what is called a Tail Hook.

The objective was to catch one of those cables with that hook; if they didn't catch it, they didn't stop. The pilot would then have to kick in all the power that jet had or fall off the side of the ship. If they went over the side, they had little chance to survive. Jets are not made to float, and the movement of the ship would suck the jet down quick.

The weather had been good when we started flying, but had become bad enough that they were cutting operations short. The Saratoga was bouncing all over the damn place, which naturally made it harder to land. The Vigilante was one of the largest aircraft to ever land on a flight deck, on a dead calm day it looked like it was falling out of the sky. The plane had to bring its air speed so low to land on an aircraft carriers deck ,that it was just above its stall speed. I got a couple pictures of the first two landings and had the camera ready to go when the third one made its approach.

What happened next put me in awe of the pilots that land jets on Aircraft Carriers. As the Vigilante crossed the Round Down, the stern of the ship lurched up, the Round Down just tipped the nose landing gear of the Vigilante and sheared it off.

The R.I.O., that's the Bomber/Navigator, mush have had his hands on the face curtain and been ready, he ejected as it happened. At the same time the Pilot pulled the nose up, and hit the After-burners. When he had pulled the nose up, the tail tilted down toward the deck, as the Vigilante passed over the last arresting wire the Tail Hook caught it. The jet stood straight up, standing on two pillars of flame, hooked to the ship by a one and one-half inch wire. The big jet was walking down the deck dragging out the arresting cable as it went. The Pilot killed the power and the jet came slamming to the deck. Momentum carried the jet till it stopped, two thirds of it hanging off the end of the angle deck.

The first thing the pilot did was stand up in his canopy-less cock-pit, and start looking for his R.I.O. He spotted him just as he hit the water, the rescue helicopter moving in for the pick up. The damn guy was setting on top of that jet like a cowboy. The only thing holding it there was the Tail Hook on the wire. As the Pilot crawled along the top of the Vigilante toward the edge of the Flight Deck, it was teetering from the heavy seas. When the pilot jumped down off the tail section onto Flight Deck, he was surrounded by guys that acted like they had just won the World Series.

It had all happened so quick, how in the Hell had that

Jet Jockey reacted to so many things going wrong in such a short period of time? I had been holding a cocked camera in my hands and did not get a picture till the R.I.O. was back on deck, standing with the pilot. Those guys not only need a little arrogance, they deserve it. I stand in awe.

I had submitted my request chit for UDT Training, and knew that it had been approved as high my Division Officer, Pappy Hayford. They had lowered the age for Training to nineteen, I still would need a waver on the age, as I would not be nineteen till well after the class I was applying for was over.

The same day I got my request chit back, approved on condition of a favorable Interview, swim, run and P.T. test, I received a letter from Mom telling me she was going to have a baby. She had to have been two months pregnant when I left on the cruise, she was to have the baby right around the time the Saratoga was due back in Long Beach. Maybe I would get a sister yet?

The world looked pretty damn good to me that day: I might get a sister, my request chit was approved , I had forty-four guys working for me on the Side Cleaning crew. That was more guys then most Chiefs on the ship had, and I was working with Good and Wolf at Flight Quarters on the Jet Fuel supply system. What more could a seventeen year old want?

My Interview and test were scheduled for our next port call in Subic Bay Philippines. There were five other

Sailors from the ship, or the Squadron that would test that day. I only new one of them, he wasn't a bad guy, just not too bright, and he didn't do any running or P.T., he lifted weight. I felt confident about the Swim, Run and P.T. Tests, but was worried about the interview, what in the hell was it about?

I asked J. D. what he thought. He was not a big help. He put a real serious look on his face, reached up and put a hand on my shoulder and said, " Karl, they have a list of questions that will identify people with a screw loose. You, young man, have at least two loose. They will spot you before you open your mouth."

I had set myself up for that. I had asked the question in our Division coffee locker with a bunch of guys standing around. Worse, the brothers strange, Wolf and Good were there. When the laughter stopped, Good said, "J. D. you got that wrong," Wolf ended it with," Ya, Karl never had any screws, he's Screw-less." Until I left the ship I was known as Screw-less.

Before pulling into Subic, we were on Joint Exercise, with the British and Australians, practicing war. The Joint Exercise ended, with everyone pulling into Subic and having a big celebration, of Queen Elizabeth's birthday. The Queen would have been horrified. Her Birthday turned into a drunken, whoring, brawl. It was the likes of which I have not since seen or even heard of.

I was to take my swimming, running, PT tests and have

my interview the morning after pulling in. So my plan was to fore go the pleasure of chasing ladies and guzzling large quantities of beer. I was going to the Navy Exchange to see a movie, then by the new Enlisted Man's Club.

My plan went astray from the start. The Navy Exchange was shoulder to shoulder with Brits and Aussies, a big line at the movie, and the huge new Enlisted Man's Club was packed to over flowing. Oh well I'd go back to the ship, eat and have a early night, was I in for a shock.

It was around 1900, 9:00 pm., and four of us were playing cards in the coffee locker when word was passed for All Hands, not in the Duty Section, to report to Hanger Bay #1. Oh crap, what now? We mustered, and found out what now. It seemed the Shore Patrol, and Police, downtown were overwhelmed with drunken Sailor, Marines and Commandos of three Nations. The Chief Masters at Arms walked through the ranks and PICKED twenty-five volunteers to assist with the problem.

We were told to report back to the Hanger Bay in fifteen minutes, in dungarees. Helmets and night sticks, would be provided. We were transported to the base Brig, on a bus that stopped and picked up Sailors and Marines from other ships. When I got off the bus, there were people all over the asphalt grinder outside the Brig. I spotted Sergeant Brooks coming out of the front door of the Brig, I got myself over there quick. If I was going to get involved in a riot or something, I wanted to be with Brooks.

It took about a half hour to get four hundred people organized, and to start moving us out. Thank God I had latched onto Brooks. We were loaded on to an old Navy bus, and taken off the base to a parking lot near the Filipino Police Station.

The whole town of Alongapo was like some DRUNKEN barroom brawl. Our job was to get the animals headed back toward the base. The Brig on the Base, and the Jail downtown were full, the only thing we could do was start on the far side of town, close bars, and drive the drunks ahead of us back toward the Main Gate.

We ended up with the job of assisting injured drunks to the First Aid station. The Corpsmen busted ass, the First Aid Station was like a war zone. We kept bringing them cut and broken people, they kept patching them up. Nine people died that night. To quote the Big Guy, "The militaries purpose is to break things and kill people." Well they did that night, just the wrong things and the wrong people.

I got back to the ship as the sun came up. The only thing on my mind was my Interview, and tests that morning at 0900, was it still going to happen? I wasn't tired, I wanted my test and that damn Interview. The whole world could fall apart, but it better not interfere with my chance to qualify for UDT Training.

I couldn't get any answers, so it was clean off the blood, stuff some food in my gut, and get myself over to the base pool, the designated testing area. I was so fired up, I was two hours early, with nothing to do but wait and worry. So that's what I did: worry about that damn Interview. I had no fear of anything on the physical side.

Brooks had told me it would be best for me if I just did what they told me, and keep my mouth shut unless they asked me something. When Chief Smidth arrived just before 0900 to administer the test, only twenty Sailors had shown up. One hundred and fifteen had been schedule to test. The weight lifter and myself were the only two, of the six, that showed up from the Saratoga. Chief Smidth had his own problems. The other two guys from UDT, that were to help him run the testing, where in the Brig.

The whole damn mess worked out good for me. When I completed my Swim Test, Chief Smidth drafted another guy and me to help him time swim test. As it worked out, I never had the dread Interview, I took each test first, then helped Chief Smidth administer the others.

Just over sixty Sailors tested that day. I was first on the Swim test, second on P.T. and twentieth on the run. At the end of that day, Chief Smidth let me know, that he was recommending me for training. All I had to do was stay out of trouble, until the next training class started, in four months.

THE TERRORIST

Now I was so damn happy I couldn't sleep if I tried. When I got back to the Saratoga, Good, Wolf and J D were in our coffee locker. We BS-ed about my test, and what had happened in town last night. The three of them had been in the duty section, and had spent the night getting drunks bedded down.

Good told me some Aussie Commando had passed out in my bunk. Wolf chimed in with, "Ya and he puked all over it too." Man those two loved to see me get it. When I groaned, they both busted up so bad I hoped they would piss their pants . They bounced around the place, cackling and slapping each other on the back.

I headed for our living space with those two on my ass. When I got to our compartment there was no mattress on my canvas bunk bottom, just a note that said:

Screw-less, We cleaned the stinky Aussie spew,

we didn't do it for love of you, but

to put you in our debt, you cheap Bastard you.

Two steak dinners, WILL DO.

It was signed Good and Better. Now it was my turn to crack up. Liberty was secured for town because of, the riots last night, but Base Liberty was allowed. I told Good and Better (Wolf), I would buy them the best steak at the new Enlisted Mans Club tonight. If I owed anyone a steak, it was Sergeant Brooks. I went down to the Marine Spaces to let him know how I had done on the test, and ask him to join us.

Well I was there both nights, the first night was bad, but if you want to use the word Riot, it should be used for the second night at the Enlisted Man's Club. Now that was a Riot! When we arrived at the Club it was already packed -- we may have gotten the last table in the place.

The Enlisted Man's Club at Subic Bay was the newest and best the Navy had. It was huge, the building held the main Enlisted Mans Club, the Acey-Duse Club for First and Second Class petty Officers and a Chiefs Club. It had big picture windows running down two walls, a big Band Stand filled another wall and a bar ran all the way down the forth.

It had been open for less than a month, and the Queens Birthday was its first true test. Sailors, Marines and Commandos, from three Nations were doing the testing, and the Club seemed to be handling the load well.

Our table sat ten, and we had a little bit of everything, British Commandos, Australian Sailors and Marines, and us good old Yanks. It had only taken thirty minutes to get our steaks. They were good meat, done right. Drinks were easy to get. You could either call a waitress, or walk up to the Bar and get as many as you could carry.

THE TERRORIST

I had a problem telling the British and Australian Sailors apart, their uniforms looked so similar. Both wore white shorts, their jumpers, there hats were similar and a lot of them had beards. There had been hardly any problems all night, a few punches traded back and forth, but in general just a good drunk being had by all.

Things started turning to shit around 2330, when they wanted everyone to leave. One of those guys in shorts with a big beard, jumped up on a table and screamed " GOD SAVE THE QUEEN." Another guy in shorts jumped up on a table and screamed "Bugger the Bloody Queen." That was it, the whole damn place went up at once.

At first I thought it was kind of funny. That is until as I got up from my chair and started to turn, some United States Marine, swung a broken beer bottle at me. I brought my left arm up, and blocked the bottle but it cut the crap out of my arm. It wasn't funny anymore, I grabbed my chair and hit the Marine and anyone else that got between me and the door I was headed for.

It was my first bad cut and all the blood flying off my arm when I swung the chair, scared me sober. When we got outside, we crossed the street and Wolf and Good took charge. Wolf set me down on the curb and grabbed a pressure point on my arm. A beer bottle makes a ugly gash, they tore up Goods shirt and bandaged my arm. Good was standing above me pointing down and laughing. “Man you should have seen yourself, swinging that chair, blood flying all over the place. You were screaming 'follow me, follow me' and hitting whoever got between you and the fucking door."

Good and Wolf had just sat down on the curb, next to me, when a table broke out the picture window that was the first to go. Drunks, the fighting men of three nations, both fighting and trying to escape, spilled out onto the grass. About an hour before everything started, Brooks had gone to the Acey-Duse part of the Club, so we didn't know where he was. Just as the second window came out, there was a big commotion, at the main door to the Club. A wedge of Marines and Sailors were forcing their way out, and in back of the wedge was Sergeant Brooks with a U.S. Naval Officer draped over his shoulder.

We took off across the street to see if we could help. Brooks didn't need us, he had it well in hand. My last memory that night was a picture window turning into thousands of pieces that exploded around me. Thirty-six hours of riot, tests, booze and loss of blood had caught up with me.

My next memory is, every cell in my body being sick at once, my mouth tasted like a heard of pigs had shit in it. My left arm was pulsating shoots of nausea straight at my gut. I had time to roll to my right and puke off the edge of my bunk, thank God for small favors. Good and Wolf, were not going to clean up this mess, it smelled worse than my mouth tasted. It took everything I had to get out of my bunk and clean up that mess. After that I didn't care about anything but getting back in my bunk and not moving for as long as possible.

It took three months and almost a million dollars to get the Enlisted Mans Club back in operation. In nineteen sixty that was big bucks. The biggest stink was caused by what happened to the Officer Sergeant Brooks had over his shoulder. He was the Executive Officer of the Naval Air Station at Subic Bay. He had just dropped by the Acey-Deuse part of the club, to buy some of his Petty Officers a drink. Brooks told me, there were no signs of what was coming, just like on our side of the Club.

As soon as the riot started, a Second Class Petty Officer hit the Naval Station Executive Officer up the side of his head, with a full beer bottle. The Officer dropped like a rock and the Second Class had started stomping him. I have no idea how in the hell Brooks put a stop to the stomping, got the Officer up on his shoulder, and organized a wedge. I mean, hell, he was right in the middle of a riot. It had been every damn thing I could do just to swing a chair!

In all the military there is no more strictly enforced rule than, you can not hit an Officer. If the military let that go, it would fall apart. Brooks not only saved the Officer's ass but he was the only one with the BALLS to identify the guy that did the deed, and testify at his Court-martial.

The Officer had been a highly respected full Commander, a top fighter pilot and the father of four. He had brain damage, so his Naval career ended as well. Now I never talked to Brooks about this, but for a colored Enlisted guy to testify against a white enlisted guy, in favor of an Officer, took BIG ONES. I don't know if he even thought about it, I'll have to ask him some day.

There were many consequences of our little international military riots! I'm sure several Senior Officers fitness reports bit the dust. People died, every ship in the Fleets of three Navies was full of walking wounded. To top it all off, every damn ship was kicked out of Subic Bay.

At the time the only thing that bothered me was losing three more nights in town, I didn't even care about the thirty or so stitches in my arm. Hey, my only excuse is, I was eighteen, which in truth is not a good excuse. I had all the tools to think things out. At the time I was just too lazy and having too good a time for serious basic thinking!.

I heal quick so it was only necessary to lay off P.T. for about two weeks. The only other thing my stitches effected was hanging nets and stages on the side of the ship -- I had to lay off that for about a week. The rest of the cruise was spent holding my breath. First, in anticipation of receiving my Orders to Underwater Demolition Team Replacement Training, then, when I received my orders, waiting for the class to start.

THE TERRORIST

It was like I was afraid the world might end before Training started. As you may have noted, during this part of my life, the rest of the world only mattered if I found it interesting. I was still fighting the truth of what One All Powerful GOD meant, I knew but didn't like it. Most of all, whenever I went digging around in my mind, Fine would turn up and I wasn't t ready to face myself on that one yet.

I must have been acting like a speed junkie, Pappy, J. D. and even Whillie were telling me things like slow down, take it easy, have a little patience. It was another time in my life when the rest of the world seemed to be in SLOW MOTION, like some giant gooey blob trying to slow me down. From experience I knew the only thing to do was just keep moving and laughing, mainly at myself. This time will pass and I don't get it back.

My Orders arrived and, low and behold, they held a surprise: I was going to Training at Little Creek Virgin instead of Coronado California. A bit unusual, in those days, Sailors on the West Coast went to Training at Coronado, Sailors on the East Coast went to Training at Little Creek. Something was up. I had no idea what but as soon as I saw were I was going to Training, two other things came to mind. They had dropped the age requirement for Training to nineteen and quickly given me a waver on the age requirement. The world I was going to was changing, I would find out how and why when I finished training.

It's funny, a little kid gets a Sailor suit, sees a movie and his whole life is on a track, a fast, interesting and difficult track. My Orders called for me to leave the Saratoga three weeks before the end of the Cruise. They had given me two weeks' leave at home, then report to the Training Facility, THANK You GOD. Only one thing reached me while I was home, Mom had the baby, we had a sister. Mom had to spend most of the time in bed, with her feet propped up. For a woman who always had things to do, it had to be tough.

She didn't do a lot of complaining, but it was obvious the not being able to work on whatever she felt was necessary, was harder then being sick. In those days you didn't find out the sex of the baby tell birth, dads weren't allowed in the delivery room,and you paid, not some insurance company. It was a different world!

I was home five days when they moved Mom to the Hospital, so most of the time it was just Jim, Steve and me. Dad was only home to change clothes and see if we had managed to wreck the place, other then that, he was at the Hospital or work. Mom would call us before Steve's bed time every night, he would be hanging around by the phone for a half hour before she was due to call.

The receiver would be off the cradle before it had a chance to ring. If it was anyone other then Mom, the normally mellow Steve would holler, "Don't call till nine thirty" and slam down the phone.

He didn't care who it was, Grandma in Michigan, Jim's friends even Dad. The first time it happened I had tried to explain that he should find out who it was and politely ask them to call back. My eight-year-old, Mr. Mellow little Brother gave me a crazed look, his lip actually had an arch in one side and it quivered, all he said was, "NO NO NO!" I was smart enough to leave it alone.

Dad called just as Steve got home from school, and asked me to put him on the line. I could tell from Dad's voice, we had a baby and everything was fine. Steve listened for a few seconds, drooped the phone and started running all around, jumping up and down and screaming “Mom's okay, we got a sister!” over and over. When I got on the phone, Dad was laughing,

Mom was great, our sister's name was Catherine Mary and I was to call everyone on the list, and let them know.

Dad called five more times that night, once from each of his best buddies' homes. He had a daughter and by God he was going to let them know himself. My dad worked hard to be the perfect man of the forties, picture that guy, that was our Dad. I had never seen him, what you might call, drunk. When Dad got home, he was funnier than hell, and couldn't walk straight. To this date, the day my sister was born is the only time I have ever thought my Dad was drunk. He still says he wasn't, but I'm a bit of an expert on drunk, and he has little experience, so I'll go with my opinion.

My Mom and sister, coming home from the hospital, got through my self-absorption. I was at least able to put training out of my mind for a few days, and get off my self-centered teenage shit. We had a few enjoyable days, the kind we had before I became a disruptive teenager. The Chief and his whole family came up the day before I left for training. They had a short visit with Mom, Dad, and our new baby girl. Then took Jim, Steve, and me out to dinner and a movie.

Those last few days of my leave before training, are very pleasant memories, and I learned a basic truth of this life. FEMALES are born different! No matter what, never let anyone convince you, that men and women are the same. If you are ever stupid enough to believe that, your relationships with women will suffer more then you can comprehend!!!

Chaos, that's the only word I can come up with, to describe what I found when I reported in at the Underwater Demolition Replacement Unit. It was housed in a bunch of ramshackle Pre-World War II buildings, stuck out of view in the far corner of the Little Creek Amphibious Base.

I reported in the afternoon before what was called," Physical Preconditioning", started. I w my class, one hundred and seventy, wannabe frogmen. As far as I as amazed by the size of knew, class size ran from 10 to 30 guys. Couple that with my age waver, and it wasn't hard to figure out something was up. It would take six months of brutal mental and physical effort to find out what.

Everyone was issued old green fatigues, and worn out boon-dockers, (old high top work shoes). The boon-dockers were nothing but harassment factors! Your feet stayed in constant pain, from running in those worn-out pieces of shit. We were told that we would receive Red Helmet if we made it through the first two weeks of training. As far as the Instructors were concerned we weren't even Trainees till HELL WEEK started.

For those first two weeks you just walked away to quit, no one seemed to notice. When Hell WEEK started they made it real easy to quit, just take your Red Helmet off. Your red helmet was our personal letter of resignation. All you had to do was take it off, and you could have a set of orders to some nice duty station, no questions ask. The day we graduated, I burned the boon-dockers, and smashed the helmet!

They called those first two weeks Physical Preconditioning, and in fact they were. The question is what condition they are Pre-ing you for. PAIN, they got every muscle in your body in the condition of pain. Their main tool for creating this pain was exercise, and your WANT A BE. If your WANT was big enough, you would BE in pain, if it was not, you quit. I heard something like this, time and time again "If this is Preconditioning, what the fuck is HELL WEEK like? I'm out of here!" Half the people that quit did it in that first two weeks leading up to HELL WEEK!

All our Instructors were Team Members, First Class, or Chief Petty Officers. From day one they informed us, we did not belong in the Teams, and they would see we didn't make it. Keep stuck in your mind, any of us could leave anytime we wanted, no penalty, no questions asked. It is the only military school I ever heard of, that you could quit, without causing yourself and your military career big problems. Our Instructors would remind us of this little fact, again and again.

Duckwalk, squat jumps, eight count body builders, push-ups, setups, squat thrust, arm circles, neck rotation, press press fling, hi Jack hi Jill, body rotations, lean and rest, hit the deck on your feet, flutter kicks, hello darlings, chin up bars, log physical training, the dread obstacle course, Mount Suribachi, and you run everywhere. In a nut shell, that was our first two weeks of training.

The first thing we learned was to assume the lean and rest. The position is fairly simple, you are on the tips of your toes and the palms of your hands, with your arms extended out from your chest. Your back must be straight, and do not let your head sag toward the ground. The hardest part, was learning to assume the position as a group.

We spent at least two hours going over the little maneuver that would get us to the lean and rest. You are standing at attention, the command, HIT THE DECK, is given. You immediately kick both feet out behind you, while sticking both arms straight and stiff in front of your chest. If you have done it properly, you land on your toes, and the palms of your hands, and are in the lean and rest.

We lost our first four men, on day one, at Mount Suribachi. It was a huge sand dune, the biggest one around, named after a mountain where thousands of marines had died in World War Two. We were introduced to the training unit's personal sand dune right after lunch that first day.

After our education in Hit the Deck, and the Lean and Rest, they had taken us for a run around the different areas we would be training in. Of course we always ran the long way, something two blocks away, was at least a three mile run. By lunch time we had run about ten miles and been introduced to all the exercises of pain that would be a big part of life in training. Damn was I Hungry.

Till Hell Week we had thirty minutes, from the time we fell out of ranks, to eat, and be back outside in formation. There was no restriction on how much food you could eat, whatever you could stuff down your throat was yours. Getting one hundred and seventy hungry guys through the chow hall in under 30 minutes, was a pure bedlam, and on that day did not happen.

When everyone was back out in formation, it had taken 45 minutes. Those of us that had been done in thirty minutes, had spent the extra fifteen minutes in a squat, duck walking. Of course since we were duck walking, we were required to quack like ducks. Many of us acquired a great dislike for some of our more laid back classmates that day.

After chow they ran us straight to Mount Suribachi. Nothing hard to learn here, you run up one side and down the other. There was one little wrinkle the Instructors would add, after HELL WEEK started, carrying sand to the top. It was an environmental thing, our Instructors had to use this sand dune for the next class, they didn't want us to wear it down.

Now this doesn't sound like it much, but the way they had us do it, was a big pain in the ass. You were required to fill your Red Helmet full of sand, hold it over your head with both hands, and run up Mt. Suribachi. If an Instructor saw you spill any sand, before you got to the top, you received some extra Instruction, something like push-ups.

On that first day at Mount Suribachi, four guys quit. Two of the guys that quit, had been the last two out of the Chow hall, GOOD RIDDANCE. With one hundred seventy trainees running, crawling, stumbling and falling all over the sand dune and one another, it was a goat fuck. I was kicked, my hands were stepped on, I fell running down hill, ending up on my face with a mouth full of sand.

I made my first friend in training, on that damn sand dune, day one. As soon as my face hit and my mouth filled with sand, a hand grabbed the back of my shirt, and jerked me up to my knees. My savior stood half way down Suribachi, holding me by the back of my shirt, while I puked sand and lunch. He kept the rest of the horde from trampling me into the side of the dune. Not a word was said, as soon as I was back on my feet, he was off and running.

One of the Instructors had seen it all. As soon as my benefactor reached the bottom of Suribachi, he was put in the lean and rest. I ran around the end of the dune and back up the far side, as I came running down, I could see my saviour doing push-ups. I have no idea why, but when I reached the bottom, I hit the deck, and started pushing Virginia away beside my unknown benefactor. The short, squat, ugly fucker just looked my way and smiled.

His name was Ronald Bertram Flacktum, always known as Shorty. Ya, that's right, the big union guy, at the time he was a Third Class Petty Officer, and a member of that undisciplined horde, called a training class. Of course I had again attracted the attention of an Instructor, who promptly began telling us what low life scum we were, and wanted to know if we were queer for each other. He sent Shorty back to running Mount Suribachi. I was given the privilege, of Duck Walking at the bottom of the dune, in the path of everyone stumbling down its side. Quack, Quack, boy was I having fun now.

We were a winter Training Class in Virginia, that meant a wide range of weather, most of it cold. In that first two weeks we had lots of rain, hail and sleet, with just a little snow thrown in. Anytime we had a chance to get dry, the Instructors would find water, sand and mud, to remedy that small measure of comfort. One of the Instructors, liked to run us down to Beach 7, and have us do push-ups in the surf. The push-ups part was no big thing, it was the cold ass water. Our oh so caring Instructor, told us he hated to make us suffer like this, so as soon as someone quits we can all get out of the surf.

Here's another thing I hate about quitters, most of them never do it when it will do anyone else some good. They would wait till that time between finishing one thing, and starting another. We must have done that push-ups in the cold ass surf twenty times, and no one ever quit, while we did it. The inconsiderate worms could have given up when it did their classmates some good.

Toward the end of the second week of training, we were assigned to our boat crews, received our Red Helmets, and our boats. The boat we would be carrying around on our heads, were Inflatable Boats Large. There were around 130 trainees at the time, so we had thirteen crews with ten members each. Having ten guys under the boat was just an added harassment factor.

In this case more was less, ten guys were to damn many. We suffered, till after Hell Week, for our inability to handle our boats in a manner that pleased our Instructors. There were guys ranging from six foot three, down to Shorty at five foot five. The guys in our Boat Crew were five nine to six one, except Shorty.

He was running around under the boat, with no weight on his head. Old Shorty showed me a quick mind in action, and a lot of class. Instead of eating, the next time we went to chow, he went in the back of the galley and rounded up a two-pound coffee can. He tied a piece of rope, to one of the rubber strap handles, on the boat. Now with the rope to hang on to, and the coffee can on top of his helmet, Shorty could carry his share of the boat.

By the end of Hell Week, every short guy that was left had a coffee can, of his own. Shorty went so far as to paint the can red, so it matched his helmet. Of course our Instructors could have made up the Boat Crews according to our size, but their business was to disrupt, not make life easy. If our Instructors had a doctrine, it was DISRUPT, AGITATE, and IMPEDE, and they were good at their jobs. When you get right down to it, that's what we were being trained for, that's what the Teams do!

If this was Preconditioning, what would Hell Week bring? I had no idea, but I wanted Hell Week now. I figured that was the fastest way to get rid of the guys that didn't belong here. For me, the shirkers, were the biggest harassment factor going, and I wanted rid of them.

These were the guys not carrying their share of the weight, they let someone else carry it. The assholes who were always late, causing the rest of us to suffer extra pain. Sergeant Brooks had been dead right, If you wanted to make it through, you weren't going to do it by yourself, or with the people who didn't pull their weight. The best example I can give you happened three days before Hell Week.

The most imposing guy in our class, was the Senior Enlisted Trainee, a First Class Petty Officer. He was six foot two, or three, and looked like he should be a Frogman. A big tough looking fucker! The only problem was, this asshole was one inch deep and a mile wide, not a bit of substance to the man.

Oh he could run, swim, and do his exercises better then most. That is, when one of the Instructors was looking. He always made sure he did the least, was in the chow hall first and out last, the first guy to point out to an Instructor, anther guys weaknesses. I was just glad the fucker wasn't in our boat crew!

To this day, I don't think even Shorty knows why he nutted up, I guess he had just had enough of the big phony fucker. We had just come back to the barracks, from a cold, wet, muddy afternoon on the Obstacle Course. I was intent on getting some dry close on, when Shorty let go. "QUIT YOU CHICKEN-SHIT FUCKER, QUIT OR I'LL KICK YOUR ASS."

I spun around and there was all five foot five of Shorty, shoving the big First Class Petty Officer out the door. We all ended up outside between the barracks, in a big circle. Looked like we were going to have a fight, and young guys love a fight. I just hoped Shorty didn't get hurt. The First Class was looking down at Shorty like he was crazy

There was no fight, the last time we saw or heard the First Class, he was stomping of through the crowd, hollering "Consider yourself On Report." In the Navy being On Report was serious business, it means you are charged with a crime. The truth was, Shorty had committed assault, against a superior Petty Officer and could end up in the Brig.

Shorty didn't seem worried at all. In fact he went back in the barracks, and dumped the First Class's clothes out of his locker. Shorty then scooped them up, and threw them out the door, on the muddy ground.,I thought my new friend was a goner. We had been given fifteen minutes to get in the barracks, change clothes, and be back in formation, in front of the Instructors hut. None of us got any dry clothes on, but for once everyone except the First Class, was in formation on time, and not a word was said.

We were taken for a three mile run, to go one mile distance, that got us to the chow-hall,. Throughout Training , if the Instructors where looking, we never took the shortest route. After chow we did the Obstacle Course, spent some time on Mt. Suribachi, and received the usual amount of physical harassment.

Most everyone figured the shit would hit the fan, when we got back to the Training Area. Not so, when we got back, nothing, well I mean nothing about Shorty and the First Class. We spent some time, in the Lean and Rest, did some Push-ups, and were dismissed.

The lazy asshole was gone, him and every trace of him. Shorty not only got rid of that First Class, but ten other guys packed their gear and quit that night. I think they got the idea that shirkers would not be put up with. All I could think was, Thank you Shorty. He had single handedly, gotten rid of more then a Boat Crew, of driftwood. Hell Week would take care of the rest!

The last two days before Hell Week were beautiful, no rain, no sleet, no snow. Both days it was a warm fifty-five degrees, with blue skies and no wind. Oh they still kept us wet, with mud puddles, ponds, canals, and the

Chesapeake Bay. Somehow just having blue skies, and air that wasn't cold, gave us all a big boost. Plus the thought, that maybe this weather would hold through Hell Week, was damn nice. Fat chance.

We had started Training with a hundred and seventy WANT TO BE frogmen, by the start of Hell Week we were down to one hundred and twenty-one. The two weeks of Preconditioning had thinned our ranks by forty-nine. We would lose another Seventy-five Trainees during Hell Week.

Guys that have completed Hell Week, have few clear memories, of those five days and nights. How it all starts is one of them. The Instructors entered our barracks, blowing whistles, banging on trash can lids, tipping over lockers, and throwing Mark-80s, a cherry bomb size explosive. The test has begun, it is two fold:
1) What is at your core?

2) Will your body break?

1) They have a simple way of testing just what is at your core, deprive you of sleep, keep you past physical exhaustion, and make you as uncomfortable as possible. When you're too tired to think, you just do what comes naturally. The Instructors make sure you understand you can leave anytime you want. That is driven home time and again, you can have a nice HOT shower, and something Warm to drink. They will be happy to get you a set of orders, to some nice warm duty station, no harm, no foul. If you don't have what it

takes, you WILL QUIT.

2) Your body is repeatedly subjected extraordinary physical strain. If it breaks, you are out. If your body heals, and you can pass the screening test, you can start Training again. One guy in our training class broke his leg two weeks from the end of training. Two training classes later, he started all over, and that time nothing broke. Getting through training once, is a feat! Getting through a second time, when you know what is coming, is an extraordinary feat.

Hell Week started as if God were on the Instructors' side, a cold driving rain greeted us, as we were flushed from our barracks. As soon as the whole Class was in formation we were told to hit the deck. Push-ups in the rain, a great way to start a week, things would go down hill from hear. The next five days and nights were cold with, rain, sleet, and a little snow thrown in for bad measure. Hell Week is one of the few things in life that lived up to their name.

No man that has gone through Hell Week can tell you much about what happened to his class. After the first, nonstop twenty-four hours, your mind is in another realm. For the last four days and nights of the week, I had a personal ghost. First Class Petty Officer Gary Fine. My murder victim, seemed to be watching me, waiting to see if I quit. Fine was an invisible, silent presence, I felt he was waiting to smile, if I quit. Not a chance I would quit , and let that lying bastard have a smile at my expense. They would have to brake my body to get me out of there.

For every participant, the week is a blur, at best. I have talked to guys, that remember nothing, after the second day. They were there, they did it, they just didn't remember anything. The best way to get a true picture of Hell Week, is go watch some other class go through it. I know of no one who has observed a complete Hell Week, it is to damn long and to the observer, boring. Who the hell wants to watch people suffer. You can only watch it in bits, and pieces. Even the Instructors are broken down into two teams, one for days, one for nights.

The trainees get to do both day and night, but then our Instructors had done it first. The Instructors have three functions; 1) Keep the pressure on. 2) Assist the quitters in getting their asses out of there. 3) Making sure that the guys that are making it don't injure themselves. Pushing motivated people to the breaking point, and not letting them injure themselves, isn't an easy task. It is not every guy in the Teams that can be an Instructor, and most of them that are Chiefs. It's odd, but a good Chief is like a good Mom, they have plenty of tough love.

For me the two things that stick in my mind with any clarity are the never ending sand and mud, and the Cargo Net on the Obstacle Course. I could understand the Cargo Net, I fell off the damn thing. Why the sand and mud bothered me so much, I still don't understand. I had spent my youth on the beach, with sand in every crack, crevice, and orifice. It had never bothered me before!

I have no idea how many times we ran the Obstacle Course that week, but I feel off the damn Cargo Net that first day. The net hung between two huge pine trees, about thirty feet apart. It was lashed, to a one inch cable, that was stretched between the trees, sixty feet up. The Cargo Net was straight forward, up one side, over the top, and down the other. I still have no idea why I fell, but it put the fear of God in me. Had I broken something, Training would have been over.

I was more than half way down the net when I fell. I had been trying to go down the net just using my hands, no feet. Sort of dropping and catching myself, a few rungs of the net down. The next thing I knew, I lay on my back, in the wet sawdust pit at the bottom of the net, with the wind knocked out of me, and my whole body numb.

I had two thoughts, I can't breath, and Fine will laugh, if I don't keep going. Before I could breath, or felt anything, I was on my feet moving to the next obstacle. Fine was helping me, whether he wanted to or not. I never tried that hand over hand shit again!

The five twenty-four hour days, of Hell Week, are a time warp, all their own. People just disappeared, days seem to repeat themselves. Cold water, sand and mud, a never ending supply of cold water, sand and mud. If they ran you till you where dry, they would find cold water, mud, and sand, no problem. Your head is driven down through your shoulders, by that damn boat. Each Boat Crew, carries their boat on there heads, everywhere, whether you are going to use it or not. Sometimes there is an Instructor in your boat, while it's balanced on your heads. I don't think anyone ever dropped an Instructor, we didn't dare.

Sometime during that week we turned into a TEAM, an us against them organism. The organism turned on the shirkers the Instructors didn't get rid of, we did it. No one would help them, not a hand, not even a nice word. You helped the helpers, not a fucking thing for those that only helped themselves. The help you got wasn't all sweetness and light, it might be a shove, or a curt, move it asshole. The last day of Hell Week, has always been called So Sorry Day, and like the rest of Hell Week it lives up to its name.

Every man wore a K-pock life jacket, big bulky World War II type, and spent most of the day crawling. One whistle blast meant, hit the deck. Two whistle blast meant, start crawling. Three whistle blast meant, get up and run. The Instructors, with help from the Team guys, had planted explosives all over the Beach 7 area and the surrounding sand dunes. You crawled, up and down sand dunes, in and out of the cold ass ocean and of course every mud hole around. Explosive going off, on all sides, sand being blasted into any exposed skin. In some ways, the Instructors had a harder day then we did. They had to keep all of their past-exhaustion trainees from being blown up.

All that last day, there is only one interruption to the crawling, THE DEATH TRAP! A truly diabolical scheme. We had just crawled off a sand dune, into a little hollow at the bottom of the dune. The class was surrounded by sand, on three sides. The fourth side faced a large pit, full of water, with big chunks of ice floating on it. Break for lunch, the dread C-rations, to my way of thinking garbage in a can. I hated the damn things! I seemed to always get Ham and Lima Beans, a truly disgusting, cold glob of grease.

That day, I was happy to have them, we had stopped crawling, and there were cigarettes in each box of C-rations. Somehow we helped each other open the small cans of food, while explosions were going off all around us. I can still remember, how good that cigarette tasted.

The object of the Depth Trap was failure, just another way to keep you cold and miserable. It was just two cables, mounted on telephone poles, one at each end of the pit. There was about six feet of space between the cables.

The bottom one was twelve feet above the edge of the pit, about fifteen feet over the water and ice. The bottom cable was fixed, tight between the two poles. The top cable was fixed at the start end, and ran through a pulley at the far end. After the cable came through the pulley, it angled down to ground level and was attached to the back of a Jeep. The whole contraption was about a hundred feet long.

THE TERRORIST

I don't know anyone that ever made it across the Death Trap! The object of course, is to cross the pit on the cables. We all knew the Instructors where going to do their best, to make sure none of us made it across. This was the fifth day of HELL WEEK, all of us were well past exhaustion, but the Death Trap is clear in my mind. No one gave up, all the QUITTERS were gone, we would fail with style.

Only three guys were allowed on the cables at a time. They kept everyone not on the wires, near the start end of the Death Trap, in a roped off area. Trainees that were not on the cables, were afforded the opportunity for extra instruction in Duck Walking, and Squat Jumping. We had an excellent view of each of our classmate's efforts. It is the first time I remember it being, us against them, the whole Class was TEAM, not a QUITTER left.

When you fell off the cables, you were to stay in the middle of the pit, and swim to the far end. You were only allowed to crawl out at that far end. Our Instructors went over that rule, again and again, they didn't want us blown up, the pit had underwater charges in it. Shorty and I were on the cables, off, and in the water together. We had made it about three quarters of the way across, our Instructors backed the Jeep up quick, and we were gone. It went that way for the whole class. The Instructors would make it hard, and if you were making it, they would make impossible.

The pride, in every man left at the end of HELL WEEK,

was not in the winning, it was in not quitting, when you couldn't win. Each HELL WEEK ends the same, they get you cleaned up, and give you a steak dinner at the chow hall. None of the participants remember, like a lot of that week, an Instructor will tell you what happened, or you will see another class going through what you did. For the next three months and one week of training, it's more of the same, but most nights you do get a few hours sleep. It was like that old Team saying, **"THE ONLY EASY DAY, WAS YESTERDAY!**

After Hell Week, no one quit, the guys we lost, were due to injury. A Medical Drop was every Trainees nightmare. Everyone had injuries of one kind or another, you did your best to keep them hidden, none of us wanted any medical types getting a good look at us.

Buy that point in training, the Instructors were the ENEMY; the only thing that stood between us and graduation. The non-stop harassment continued, while we had classes in: Hand-to-Hand Combat, Small Boat Training, Distance and Survival Swimming, Intelligence Collection and Dissemination Techniques, Communication, Inland Penetration Raids, Basic Electric and Non-Electric Demolition Techniques, Lifesaving and First Aid Techniques, Land Navigation, Day and Night Patrolling, Survival, Escape and Evasion, Combat Firing Methods, Use of Hand Grenades, and Surf Penetration, which was saved for storm Surf days.

In Hand-to-Hand Combat classes we would learn some

quick and quiet kill techniques that would stick with me for life. My three kills up to that time, had all involved a bang of some type. I learned two parts of the neck that offered quick quiet kills, where the spine ties into brain, and the windpipe. The Garrote, an amazing little tool, that can be made from your belt, light cord or wire. You can go from a not one sound strangling with a wide belt, to a slice the head off quick death, with a 24 inch long wire between two handles.

Now breaking the neck is pretty damn easy, but is not quite as silent a kill technique as the Garrote. If your victims lungs are full, there will be a fairly loud groan as he dies. That first day in Hand-to-Hand Combat Class, I was given an up close and personal demonstration on the impossibility of the victim getting out a sound, when the Garrote is applied correctly.

After our instructors had completed the first demonstration of the Garrote, on each other, using a Gae Belt as a Garrote. It's a two inches wide, soft cotton belt that holds your Karate uniform closed. We were ask if we had any questions. My hand was one of several hands that went up, I was called on first, my question: " Can the victim get a scream out?"

I was told to stand in the middle of the room and get out any sound I could. Well when they were done with me that questions was answered. I was given five opportunities, and each time the belt ended up around my neck, just tight enough to stifle any sound, and cutoff any intake of air. With just the slightest bit more pressure, I would have been dead without a sound, each of those five tries. I guess each of my classmates had had the same question, because when they were done with me, no one ask any more questions.

Another nice little move that I learned was what I like to call " The Two Finger Tracheotomy". Take your thumb and forefinger, now feel that spot just above the middle of your throat where they can easily slip in behind your windpipe. Now give a little squeeze. I think you can understand how effortlessly your windpipe could be ripped out with just a thumb and finger.

These weak spots in the human structure, would give me several quick and quiet kills over the years. Mainly because I have practiced the moves time and time again since that first class.

The biggest shock in training, for many of us, was at the end of the first four months. It was like a switch was flipped, we went from, a non-stop magnitude of exertion that is generally not even matched in combat, to Army Jump School, for us a cake walk. It was like we had been running twenty-six miles everyday for four months, and suddenly we were only running four. The next two months, three weeks of Jump School, and five of Underwater Swim School, were no physical strain. Funny the only problem for many of us, was the level of academic standards required to get through Underwater Swim School.

THE TERRORIST

My biggest problem in all of Training, was physics! Now you might think, as I did, WHAT IN THE HELL DOES A UNDERWATER WARRIOR NEED WITH PHYSICS? I finally came to think of Physics, as part of Gods' laws for life. If a diver doesn't stay in lock step with Gods' laws of Physics, they are crippled or dead.

Thank God for my classmates, they kept the pressure on. By that I mean, our classmates did not give those of us that were slow, a minute’s peace until we got it. A small example might be: I'm sitting in the Tomato Patch, a Key West bar, trying to pick up a fine looking lady. Shorty will not leave me alone, till I recite both Boyle’s, and Henry's Laws. And no she wasn't interested in a guy that could recite Henry's and Boyle's Laws.

Graduation Day was an odd day, we had pulled each other through the last six months, now we were being split up into the two East Coast Teams, 21 and 22. They have to split up training classes, no one in the class knows when to stop, but you don't realize that at the time. It takes a good six months at least, before most guys' judgment starts to function properly. You have to learn to quit, if it will get the job done.

Frogman/SEAL

We had a briefing after graduation that finally explained why our training class had been so damn large. A new, Top Secret, team had been formed called, SEAL Team. SEAL stood for Sea, Air, and Land. President Kennedy had been asked by the CIA, for a new small military outfit to work with, on Special Operations. Kennedy being a former sailor, gave the job to the Navy. They had formed a SEAL Team on each coast, SEAL Team 1 in Coronado California, and SEAL Team 2 at Little Creek Virginia. Each team consisted of, just over 100 people, they were made up of volunteers from Under Water Demolition Teams.

All top flight experienced people, of course this left U. D. T. short handed, hence our large training class. It was why we were required to complete Jump School, and why we had to attend Underwater Swimmers School. After the briefing, the teams had a get to know each other, Keg Party. For the next eight years, that I was in the Teams, there would be at least one Keg Party every week.

In those days, the unofficial rule, was WORK HARD, PLAY HARD. A bunch of us were standing around a picnic table, just shooting the breeze. Up walks one of the older Team guys, he sets down a water class, full of clear liquid, on the table, and throws out a challenge: " I'll pay for any ones drunk this weekend, that can drink that water glass straight down, without puking." Before anyone else could make a move, I had that glass up, and was slamming it back. Well I didn't puke, but it knocked me to my knees, made my eyes water, and took my breath away.

I had acquired my new Sea Daddy, the perpetrator of this little drinking feat, Jimmy Henily. He was a Second Class Petty Officer and a plank holder in the newly formed SEAL Team. Jimmy must have been all off 25 years old, he was a hard working, hard partying Irishman, who always new where the line was. I wish I could tell you Jimmy taught me were the line was but till I learned to handle booze that was impossible. For the next nine years of my team career, I would cross the line many times, most times behind booze.

Henily was a regular looking guy, sandy hair, 5' 11", maybe 170 pounds. He had three things going for him, that made Jimmy one of the most liked guys in the Teams;

(1) He was a hell of an operator, Jimmy took everything the Teams did with deadly seriousness.

(2) If a piece of equipment was needed, and it could not be gotten through normal (legal) channels, he could get it. I don't care if it was a Keg of Beer, or a Stoner Weapons System, Jimmy could get it.

(3) The son of a bitch, loved to have fun. Fun for Jimmy meant work hard, do a good job, then party hardy.

After that first Keg Party, on Graduation day, I would never see some of my Classmates again. Each coast had at least two UDTs, and one SEAL Team. Each Team had five platoons, four operating and one headquarters. In those days an operating platoon was 14 men divided into two seven man fire-teams.

There was at least one platoon from each Team, away on some deployment at all times. Other platoons would be away on some training operation. Individuals were coming and going from every kind of school imaginable: Ranger School, Jungle Warfare, Language School, Outboard Engine School, Parachute Rigging School, the list went on and on. As much as was going on at the Teams, it was a slow down from training. To those on the outside it seemed that we maintained a hectic pace, for us, it was a cake-walk.

We lost our first Teammate, and Classmate within a month of graduation. Ray Halls, the best long distance runner in our class, died after a long run. Ray was assigned a platoon leaving Little Creek the day after graduation, for operations in the Caribbean.

I think if he hadn't been so fast he might be alive today. They were operating off the Island of Vegas, living in a nice encampment down by a beach. Everyone in the platoon went on a twenty mile run, Ray was the first one back. When the other guys started coming in, Ray was beyond first aid. He had died of Heat Prostration, it didn't pay to be a winner that day

There was no misunderstanding about death, it was respected, but not feared. It was the same in the Teams, as in training, you could leave anytime you wanted. So if one of us died, we did it doing what we wanted to be doing. For most of us, that's the way it was and not a bad way to go!

The Teams were unique in the military at that time, a world unto itself. Demanding in an operational sense, but forgiving of personal failures, that would end careers in other military units. The truth of the matter is, for nine years, I was always on the edge, one step away from being thrown out of the Teams, and a couple times the navy. One of my infractions caused me to spend a year in the fleet, and at that I was damn lucky.

There was never an operational problem, all of my problems came from liberty, and booze. I was where I wanted to be, but was having a lot of problems learning to handle myself within the loose demands made on my personal life. Well we all have our cross to bear, mine was myself.

Those years in the Teams, were the fastest years of my life. I guess I can sum them up best, as a graduate course in the human condition. So much was going on, so much information about myself and the rest of the human race was coming in. My problem was, I didn't take the time to step back and think about it. I could write fifty books, just about the guys that made up the Teams, maybe I'll do that after I turn myself in. For now I'll give you a quick tour, of just what brings my strange mind into focus.

Rarely will you ever hear a Team guy call himself a SEAL. He'll say something like I'm in the Teams of I'm a TG. Which of course mens Team Guy! I will tell you flat out there are no better fighting men on this earth.

I believe it's harder living with in the Teams then getting even getting through Training. TG are demanding of each other and never let the pressure off.

THE TERRORIST

One thing you need to understand the Teams are a Brotherhood! A Green Brotherhood.

My Green Brothers!

You ask who are my Green Brothers?

First here's who they are not.

They are not of one hight or weight.

They are not of one religion or race.

They are not of one political party,

nor economic class.

They are never politically correct.

Most important, they are not quitters.

Now think on this, this is who they are.

They will go to the edge and beyond, alone or as a group.

When knocked down, they get back up

and keep getting back up,until they win.

When they have nothing left, they find more and share it.

They stand ready to do the Bad Business of War.

They are my Teammates.

Yesterdays Frogmen, Todays SEALs.

John Carl Roat

Class-29, UDT-21, UDT-11, SEAL Team 1

You would think that as hard as I had worked to get to the Teams, I would follow the rules, not so. I pulled a fast one on the Teams and our esteemed federal government right from the first day I reported to the Teams. Just to be accepted for Training you have to fill out the paper work for a Confidential Clearance.

This was the lowest form of security check, and you had to pass it before they issued you your orders. I hate paperwork, but if I hadn't filled it out, no matter how well I did on my Test, I wouldn't have received orders to Training.

Well the first day we reported to Teams they gave each of us a huge stack of paper, and told us to fill it out for a Secret Clearance. I had one thought, SHIT, and when no one was looking, I threw that large stack of paper in the trash.

In over eight years in UDT and SEAL Teams, I was asked about my Secret Clearance twice. Once, right after I Shipped-over (Re-enlisted), they asked me where my Secret Clearance was. I told them I had no idea, so they gave me a new stack of bullshit papers to fill out, which I of course promptly trashed canned.

The second time it was ever mentioned, was when I was getting out of the Navy. Now that one caused a bit of agitation! I had been in the Teams for nine years, the last six a member of SEAL Team, the most Secret Unit in the Military. That was one time that I damn near got busted for not having a Secret Clearance. I'll tell you about that a little further on, I think it will point out how weak security truly is. When every you think of security think: Security My Ass!

Diving, demolition and jumping out of planes were basic major skills, that were constantly being polished . Most of the guys in the Teams took what we did pretty serious, but few were as serious about their equipment as Henily , I took my cue from him. My Sea Daddy had a simple philosophy, FUCK THEM, HURRAY FOR US!

Jimmy said most people lost out of habit, they knew how to be losers, they were a success at it. It was easy to pick these people out, they always had an excuse, nothing was their fault. " Karl you don't have to be the best to win, you just have to keep getting up when knocked down!"

I got to see a fine example of the Henily Philosophy in operation, my third month in the Teams. Jimmy couldn't box worth a shit, but he became the Heavy Weight Champ of the Navy. He had one thing going for him, it was impossible to knock the son of a bitch out. All year the Navy holds tournaments all over the world. By the time my Class graduated into the Teams, Jimmy had already won a total of twenty fights. He had to win three more fights to get to the Championship Tournament, being held on our base that year.

I didn't get to see any of Jimmy's fights till the Championship, as all three were held on other Bases. I just knew that he won, and all my Teammates though it was funny. I was in for a shock.

In those days, head gear for amateurs was optional, but most guys wore it. It softened any blow to the head, and of course lessened the chance of being knocked out. Well our man Henily didn't wear it, not only that, he would never block an opponents punch. For the first two rounds he would stand right in front of his adversary, and take any punch they could hit him with.

SEAL Team was Top Secret, so Jimmy couldn't even fight under his own unit's name, he was listed a s a member of Underwater Demolition Team-21. The Championship Tournament lasted three days, and to become Champ of your weight class, you had to win one fight each day. At a 170 some pounds, Jimmy was the smallest guy fighting as a heavy weight. In an odd way he was the main attraction. Like me, most of the fighters at this tournament had never seen Henily fight, they had heard, but never seen.

All can I say is it was bizarre, every guy from the Teams that could get there did. Some guys that were away on detachment even got back, not all in a legal way. Now Jimmy being in the Teams and loved as he was, you would think we would be cheering him on.

Not so, before each of his fights, the Teams went into a Kill Henily Chant. Before he and his opponent entered the ring we would stomp our left foot, Kill Henily, stomp, Kill Henily, stomp Kill Henily. With close to 100 guys there, from all three Teams, we rocked the place. When Jimmy entered the ring every one started booing, like telling an actor to break a leg before they go on stage.

Looking at Jimmy enter the ring, you would have though he had not a care in the world. We were all booing him, his opponent was dancing around the throwing punches, and Henily was acting like he was going to the store. The guy he was fighting, out weighted Jimmy by about 25 pounds, and had a four inch reach advantage. The big guy had on head gear, Jimmy none, the big guy could box, Jimmy couldn't, or maybe it's, didn't, I'm not sure.

I saw him fight six times, it went the same every time. The first two rounds Henily would stay in close, never backing up or blocking any of his opponents punches. The only punches Jimmy threw were body punches, he didn't do a lot of bobbing and weaving, just working the guys body and taking a lots of head shots. Henily was knocked down at least once in every fight I saw.

When he would get knocked on his ass, all of us would go crazy stomping our feet, and grunting like gorillas. Jimmy would bounce back to his feet before the referee could start his count. He would stand there with his gloves held up to his chest and that not a care in the world look on his face; his eyes glued to his opponent.

Round three would belong to Jimmy, by then his adversary had hit him with everything he had, to no effect. It was as if they just gave up, Henily would chase them around the ring, pounding them with overhand rights, his only good punch. Four of the fights I saw, Jimmy knocked them out, the other two the Ref. Stopped the fight.

His fights were always ugly, no sweet science there, just take every punch they could throw then club them into submission. In a way, Henily fights were like training, keep taking it till they quit, you win!

My first school after reaching the Teams, was to be Army Rigger School, Fort Lee Virginia. I still had not acquired a taste for jumping out of a perfectly good Airplane. The main reason being, it wasn't clear to me how, and why, parachutes worked.

Well Jimmy Henily took care of that, he had me packing his Sport Parachutes, well before I went to school. It amazed me how quickly I learned to pack a chute, Henily showed me once, and watched me twice, after that I was on my own.

When explained, the simplicity and elegance of how a Parachute operates is easily understood. Jimmy was jumping the chutes I had packed, a big boost for my status in the Teams, if Henily trusted me, I was accepted.

The only thing I found odd about Henily was his absolute passion for history. I mean hell he had a whole room of hardback books, some of them very old. Jimmy was always quoting one dead guy or another, and saying things like "Those that don't know history are domed to relive it". I would ignore his suggestions to "read a little history" until I spent one strange night hidden under the floor of a shack listening to some fake Communist Indoctrination.

In an odd way Jim is responsible for me becoming what I am, If I had never studied history, I wouldn't have seen the need for what I'm doing.

About half the young guys in the Teams were involved in civilian Sky Diving, a fairly new sport in those days. You couldn't use military parachutes, you had to have your own, a big expense. There was one way around spending $400.00 for a civilian parachute, get one of the Teams Riggers to make you one. One hundred to hundred and fifty bucks would do the trick. They were made out of old surveyed military parachutes, that could be bought for fifteen dollars. Army Rigger School would make me a financially independent sailor.

You learned all kinds of unnecessary shit , for the Teams, at Fort Lee: How to drop a tank, low level cargo extraction, building combat expendable platforms, things we would never use. One thing you did learn, was how to use a Singer 3115 sewing machine.

A magic money maker, not only could you modify parachutes, you could tailor baggy military uniforms, sew on rank and unit patches, and charge money for all of it. For the eight years I was in the navy after Army

Rigger School, I banked every pay check, and lived off that Singer 3115.

Two of the schools I attended, that affected my approach to this special form of terrorism, where S.E.R.E. and J.E.S.T. Acronyms for SURVIVAL, EVASION, RESISTANCE & ESCAPE and JUNGLE ENVIRONMENTAL SURVIVAL TRAINING. These two schools would change my outlook on the human race, and set me on the path of learning as much of history as I could. Which of course led to my practicing this strange form of terrorism .

S.E.R.E. was an inter-service school, run by the Navy. It was designed to familiarize people holding SECRET clearances with survival and escape techniques, as well as Communist style prisoner of war camps. The school was a week long, the first two days were about living off the land, and Sneak and Peek. It was all classroom and in the field demonstrations, with no harassment. Then you were turned lose in a semi-arid area of the Great State of California, for a couple days of fun and games. Your objectives; stay clear of the instructors, and feed yourself off the land.

Just a couple of small problems for the students: 1) The area had been picked clean by all the previous classes. 2) The instructors knew every nook and cranny for miles around. If you were caught, you were sent straight to a prison compound patterned after a Korean War communist prison camp. If you managed to stay clear of the Instructors, you still had to turn yourself in at the end of two days. The guys that managed to stay clear, and get themselves to the designated surrender area, were given a sandwich and a couple pieces of fruit. You then joined your captured S.E.R.E. classmates in the prison compound.

There were about two hundred and fifty students in the course, five of us were from the Teams. Two enlisted men from SEAL Team 2, two enlisted men from UDT-11 and an officer, Lt. Commander Ryan.

Ryan's nickname was Irish, he was 6'6" with red hair and freckles. This guy was a by the book Naval Academy Graduate, that would one day be the first Admiral, out of SEAL Team. More important to me, he would save my ass from Portsmouth Naval Prison, and a Bad Conduct Discharge.

For us Team guys, the school was a cake walk, but most of our classmates were office types that handled Secret Information, or technicians and mechanics that worked on Secret equipment. The majority of these guys were from the navy or air force, and had no experience of this kind of shit. At the indoctrination we had all been told that if you didn't pass this school you would loose your Secret Clearance. Since I didn't have one, I thought that was damn funny.

To not pass you had to confess to war crimes, rat on your fellow prisoners, or join the Communist Party. Of course there had been Team guys through S.E.R.E. before, so all you had to do was ask a few questions around the Teams and you knew what to expect. We all knew they couldn't drill our teeth, or poke us with Cattle Prods, I couldn't figure how they could get anyone to fail. Dumb me, I had no idea how easy it would be!

I have to hand it to Irish Ryan, we never called him that to his face, it was Lt. Commander Ryan, or YES SIR, they never caught the big lanky fucker, he was the last guy to turn himself in. Little did our commie friends know, what we had been up to, for the two days of living of the land.

They should have been watching their empty Prison Camp! A mass escape was all set up, it would happen within three hours of Irish being brought into the compound. Commander Ryan had given each of us Team guys four Direct Orders before reporting to school.

Order # 1: Follow the rules of the school, we would beat them at their own game using the holes in their established rules.

Order # 2: Stay away from each other during the indoctrination. Keep a very low profile.

Order # 3: We were to rendezvous with Commander Ryan, at a spot yet to be determined, within one hour of being turned loose on the survival course. Pay close attention at the Indoctrination, he would get the word to us then.

Order # 4: You are to do everything possible, to assist all our classmates in passing this school, and escaping from the prison camp.

After giving us Order # 4, Commander Ryan had looked me straight in the eyes, waited about ten seconds and said "Austin I know your history, do not stir any shit, unless I give you an Order to do so, or it assists our classmates." All I could say was, "Yes Sir." Oh well, there went my plans out the window.

Irish Ryan may have been a by-the-book pain-in-the-ass, but he was one smart customer. During our Survival Phase he had seen we ate well, and setup the Prison Compound for a mass escape. For a by-the-book guy, he had a devious mind. Ryan could find the holes in the rules, quicker then most people could spout them.

During the briefing for the Survival Phase Commander Ryan had asked a few questions. One of them, he had gotten up and pointed to a location on the training area map, about two miles from the starting point. BINGO, he had communicated our rendezvous point, a dry wash on the edge of the training area.

Letting two hundred and fifty inexperienced survivalists, loose in an area three miles wide and twelve long, was a joke. None of us from the Teams, had talked with each other, since our arrival at the Survival Training area. We wore no unit patches, or name tags on our fatigues, and had let none of the other students know what unit we were from. The Instructors all new that there were guys from the Teams in the class, Commander Ryan had just not wanted them dwelling on the fact. Plus he didn't want the rest of our classmates trying to hook up with us, and slow us down.

When they let us go, I took off at a dead run, doing my best to get clear of my classmates. The sun would be setting in about thirty minutes, so I ran about three miles, in the opposite direction from the indicated rendezvous point. There was another dry wash that intersected with one where we were to meet. When I was in the bottom of it, no one could see me, unless they were down there with me, or were on the lip looking down. Now I had a way to my shipmates, which was hard to observe. The dry wash made a gully about twelve feet deep that varied from five to twenty feet wide.

Everyone had understood Commander Ryan pointing at the map, we all reached the rendezvous point. I stayed on the lip of the gully, doing look out duty, as Irish briefed our Teammates. We were going on the attack, I was going straight to the prison camp with Lt. Commander Ryan. The other three would keep pace with the main body of the class. Their job was to harass the Instructors, make it as easy for our classmates to get to the end of course, as possible. They were given only two restrictions, they could not destroy any Government Property, or leave the boundaries of the Training area. The fun was on!

Ryan had asked no questions about the Prison Camp, we could all see it plainly marked on the map, within the Survival Training Area. He and I were going to get to the Prison Camp as quickly as possible, Recon the place, and make our plans. We had ten miles, as the crow flies, over broken ground, to get in the area of the Prison Camp. To our advantage, we had the dark, and a plan of operation that the Instructors rarely faced.

While Irish and I were on our little cross country Sneak and Peek, our Teammates were wreaking havoc with the Instructors' capabilities of harassing our classmates. About a half mile from where we had our rendezvous, they came upon one of the Instructor's trucks. They did a little scouting around, and located the Instructors, waiting in ambush about a quarter mile away.

They didn't break anything on the truck, but by God they screwed it up. They let the air out of all four tires, and removed the rotor cap. Our boys took the jack, rotor cap, a couple cases of the Instructors C-Rations from the truck, and beat feet.

By the time Irish and I reached the Prison Camp, our guys had done the same thing to three other trucks. They took the rotors and jacks, from all four trucks, back to the Survival Training Headquarters, and left them in the back of a pick up truck. Of course they let the air out of all four tires. The two cases of our Instructors' C-Rations, they found in the back of the truck, were appropriated. As any good Robin Hood would do, they used those two cases to help feed some of our very hungry classmates.

It had only taken Irish and me, less than three hours, to cover the ten miles from our rendezvous point to the Prison Camp. We had done it, at a low profile dog trot, not a stealthy Sneak and Peek. Hoping our Instructors, would not be looking for us this deep in the Survival Training Area, we had been in luck. There was only one little light on in the Prison Camp Area. It was on the porch of the Administration Building, and shed no light into the Prison Camp itself. Because our Teammates, had incapacitated the Instructors' trucks, they couldn't transport any captured students. That gave us all night to do a reconnaissance, and get done, whatever would expedite escape from the camp.

The prison compound was basically two 18 foot wire fences, topped with barbed wire, one inside the other. The inner compound was the main prison, and about the length of a football field, and three quarters as wide. The outer fence on three sides was twenty feet from the inner, no vegetation, and at night well lit. On the fourth side the fences were one hundred feet apart, and held the two gates, one in each fence.

Right in the middle of the fourth side, between two fences was a 20 foot by 20 foot building set on blocks, about a foot and a half of the ground. There was one twenty-five foot watch tower on each side of the compound, with flood lights, to keep everything well lit at night.

Commander Ryan gave me the towers, and both fence perimeters to Recon. He would take all the out buildings, and the power supply, we would both do the interior separately. We took longer on our Recon than we had getting to the Prison Camp. We met twice, during the reconnaissance, letting each other know what we were finding. I thought I was pretty sneaky, but Irish, Mr. by- the -book himself, put me to shame.

Each Guard Tower had an air cooled 30 caliber machine gun, with four hundred belted blank rounds. Now Blanks Rounds won't hurt anyone, but just the sound of automatic weapons going off, will stop a lot of people in their tracks. Irish had me remove the bolts, take the firing pin out, and replace the bolts. He had me give him, all four firing pins, after everything came down, we would have to give them back.

If they checked out the weapons without firing them, they would never know something was wrong, till it was too late. While I was doing that, he was running some wire he had found in the maintenance shop. Commander Ryan's" degree was in Electrical Engineering, he sure put his knowledge to good use that night.

Irish ran one wire, from the two-twenty supply in the shop, under the fence. He ran one from the 110 supply, and one wire from the loud speaker. They all ran side by side, buried in a six-inch trench, coming from the shop, to the bottom of the fence post, at the Southwest corner of the inner compound.

Irish had the bare wire, on the end of each, covered with a plastic insulator. All you had to do was uncover the ends of the wire, remove the insulators, and touch the three ends together. Every circuit in the place would blow, the lights would be out, and the P.A. System would be gone.

We next snipped wire on the Northwest end of the Camp, not the inner compound wire, but the outer. Irish figured, they wouldn't look at the outer wire as closely. He had me cut strands close to two poles. I cut from the bottom, up for about two feet up. When both poles were done, it made a flap we could fold up. I straightened and dirtied the ends, so our work would be harder to detect. The wire snipes were courtesy of our Instructors work shed, and Irish wasn't done with them yet. He buried them in the dugout closest to the North end of the Camp, where he could get his hands on them when necessary. Ryan's" plan was set, and fairly simple.

The operation would commence, the first night that everyone was in camp, as soon as possible, after full dark. We would short out the lights and the loud speaker system, cut a hole in the inner fence, and get as many of our classmates out as we could. When you figure only five guys were in on it, but one hundred-thirty-two would escape, it was a damn successful operation. We covered our tracks as best we could, stole one case of C-rations and headed into the hills north of the Prison Camp.

It was 0500, by the time we cleared the Prison Camp, we had thirty-six-hours till we had to turn ourselves in. I figured it was hide out, and kick back time. Believe me, Commander by-the-book Ryan, kept my ass hopping! Oh well, time flies when you're having fun. We set up three look out posts, small hidden areas where we could monitor the prison camp, around the clock.

We never stayed in one too long, put it back to nature's way, and move to the next. Irish wanted every bit of Intelligence we could gather, before we turned ourselves in. The next thirty-six hours were, sleep an hour, watch an hour, and an hour moving. By the time we turned ourselves in, we knew they hadn't discovered any of our preparations, and how the whole place operated.

Irish had me turn myself in thirty minutes before the deadline. He surrendered at 1700 on the dot. Commander Ryan wanted everyone in the prison camp when he arrived. From the minute he entered the prison camp, they were on Irish like wet on rain. The compound was a nut house, all the Instructors were wearing Communist Uniforms, and running everyone around like a bunch of chickens with our heads cut off. None of the officers would step forward and take charge, I guess they didn't want to come to the instructor's attention. When Irish got there, that all changed.

It was funny, I mean laugh out loud, funny. The head

Commie was about five foot six, he and Ryan, were just inside the gate. The Commie was screaming and slapping. The little bastard would grab six foot six inch Irish Ryan by the collar and try to pull his face down. When that didn't work, he would jump up and slap his face. It looked like something out of a stupid movie.

Irish was the senior officer there, and as soon as the make believe Commie, turned him loose in the compound, he took charge. His first move was to gather all the officers and senior non-commissioned officers in the far corner of the compound and set up a Chain of Command. The Commies didn't want a Chain of Command, they wanted an inventory. Each man was going to receive a number and a little public humiliation, Officers first. They ordered Irish to have all the prisoners in formation at the south end of the compound, in front of a little hill with a communist flag on it.

The fun began. We had been standing to attention for about five minutes when the commies caught the first guy wiggling. There were six of them moving through the ranks, if you moved, did anything but keep your body to attention and eyes straight ahead, you were shoved to your knees, screamed at and repeatedly slapped. This little farce went on for about a half hour. Then the head commie gave us a thirty minute lecture on, "The true history of Capitalism. It's failures, and the glory of the people's worldwide communist movement."

They moved all our officers over by the fence and had them strip down to their underwear, just bottoms. Then they placed them on their knees, on both sides of the Communist Flag, facing the ranks. We were instructed that the Capitalist Pigs kneeling in front of us were no longer our officers. We were to address them and everyone else as comrade. We were all equal now.

They had the rest of us move over to the fence, and take everything off but our underwear. We were then told to start four lines, ten feet in front of four chairs that had been set up near the flag. Well due to my lifelong habit of not wearing underwear, there I stood with the pimples on my butt for the whole world to see. I was twelve guys back, in line number two. There were four, what they called Commissars, one in each chair. They had six of the commie fuckers, going through our clothing over by the fence.

Each man had to drop to his hands and knees, and crawl the ten feet, to the Commissar, when called forward. You had to kneel there, give them your name, rank, and serial number. They would check you off a list, and assign you a number. Each man was told not to use his name again. You were to answer to Comrade and your number only.

When I came to the head of my line, the shit it the fan. All four Commissars were out of their chairs, screaming things like degenerate, CAPITALIST PERVERT. They lost it, there was a lot of screaming, and a little slapping. I was on my knees, with all four of the Commissars, screaming down at me and slapping at my head. Irish Ryan inserted himself in the mess, and of course he was punished for his act. I was told to get to the fence, put on my pants and get back in line.

Fuck them, I didn't just put on my pants, I put on everything and walked over and mingled with the fifty or so guys who already had their numbers. No one paid any attention. All four Commissars were standing over Irish, screaming and slapping.

My simple little act of not getting a number, would throw the whole prison camp into confusion. They ended up one man short. They knew it was Karl Austin, but they had no idea which of us was that was. By checking their turn-in records, from the Survival Phase they could see I should be in the camp. To their way of thinking, the only other possibility was, I had already made an escape.

I had talked with Commander Ryan about what I had done, as soon as the Commissars had turned him loose. He was about to pull off a mass escape, and I didn't want my actions to screw it up. Irish Ryan's personal order to me, was fresh in my mind. "Austin I know your history, do not stir any shit, unless I give you an Order to do so, or it assists your classmates!" He gave me, the go ahead, to keep the confusion going as long as I could.

You were considered to have escaped, when you had gotten outside both fences without being caught. There was one hard and fast escape rule, if you got out of the

Prison Camp, you had to turn yourself in, within 30 minutes. That way they didn't have to send Instructors to look for you. If you had not turned yourself in after 30 minutes, they had to consider you injured, and start a search.

After turning yourself in you would be given a sandwich and a couple pieces of fruit. The same shitty sandwiches they had passed out, for not getting caught, during the Escape and Evasion phase. When I didn't turn myself in after 30 minutes, they sent some Instructors out to find me. They also started slapping Commander Ryan around again, wanting him to tell them, where I was.

Their biggest problem in locating me was, they had already begun moving people out of the main compound. They had three other areas, all designed to get you to screw up; (1) The Indoctrination Building (shack), in the outer compound. (2) The Interrogation Center, outside the compound. (3) The Red Cross Center, outside the compound.

That's where they would get a picture of me standing in front of a Commie flag, with my right hand up, like I was swearing to something, they had tricked my dumb ass. They had some of our classmates in each area of the school.

The Commies had made it really easy at first. They would gather up guys in little groups and ask your number. All I did was give them a phony number, and hope for the best, I got lucky three times. They finally busted me, by bringing everyone back into the main compound and having us line up in ranks by number. When they started, bringing everyone back into the Inter-Compound, Command Ryan told me to give myself up as soon as everyone was in Ranks.

It was just after full dark, 20:00 or 8:00 P.M., when they finally had their hands on, yours truly. They kept everyone in ranks, so they could witness me, suffering the repercussions of my actions. I was placed on my knees, on a little knoll, in front of my classmates. Four Commies were screaming and shouting, one of them was doing a little slapping.

I'm sure It looked a lot worse then it was. I endeared myself to our feature Admiral forever, after few minutes of this penny anti-shit, all four instructors', needed to take a breath at the same time.

When they did, I hollered out as loud as I could, "IF THAT'S THE WORST YOU COMMIES FUCKERS GOT, YOU BETTER STAY AWAY FROM MY MOM." They had lost control, everyone in the ranks busted up laughing. They quickly dismissed the ranks, and went back to work on me. It was Kaka time, Commander Ryan struck!

While they were venting their anger, on little old me, Irish had the other three Team guys start a fight at the north end of the camp. When everyone's attention was directed on the fight or me, he unburied the wires and blew every circuit in the place. Three things happened in quick succession: 1) The lights brightened. 2) The P. A. System screamed. 3) Every light in the place blew.

I was up, off my knees, and gone in a heart beat. My job was to secure the main gate, and stir shit for as long as I could. Irish already had the cutters, he cut the hole in the inner fence, went through and lifted the wire on the outer fence. Our Teammates guided as many of our classmates, as they could get their hands on, through the fences.

My task at the gate had been easy, none of the Instructors had tried to get in or out. For the first few minutes they didn't seem to know what to do By that time, over half the class was in the woods, and to my mind, the Instructors surrendered. They had given everyone a word, ADMINISTRATIVE. The word was only to be used, when it was necessary to stop training, and restore normal Military Order.

ADMINISTRATIVE, ADMINISTRATIVE! Our Instructors were all running around in the dark, screaming administrative. Not even the Thirty Caliber, blank adapted, machine guns, worked. They had lost control of not just one or two of us, but the whole damn class! It took an hour, just to get everyone back in the compound, and another two hours to get the lights functioning. Of course Irish and I, would become the focus of our Instructors anger and embarrassment, but that would backfire on them too.

Since none of us Team guys had escaped ourselves, we

were still in our Instructors hands. The head Commie had taken a quick inventory, of the remaining Prisoners, they had a lot of sandwiches and fruit to pass out. Their primary concern had to be making sure everyone got safely back into the prison compound. Their secondary concern was to regain control of their school, from us.

Concern #1, was of no difficulty, everyone who had escaped turned themselves back in within thirty minutes. They were hungrier then hell, if they wanted their food they had to follow the rules, and turn themselves in.

Concern #2, would be handled by removing all five of us Team guys from the general population, until they were back in control. Commander Ryan and we four cohorts, were taken to the Interrogation Center, just outside the outer compound.

It was a long, narrow building just outside the fence, on the west end of the compound. Three quarters of the building were taken up with twenty small interrogation rooms, on each side of a central hall. The far end of the building was a big room where the BOXES were. The Box, was patterned after a communist form of torture, in which a prisoner was crammed into a small metal box, and left there, for long periods of time.

There was one main reasons that the box couldn't be as effective for our fake Commies, as it was for the North Koreans: They could only leave us in there for short periods of time. The North Koreans could let them shit and piss all over themselves, till they died, or talked! I have a suspicion, that by that time a couple of our fake commie Instructors, would have liked to try that one, on us Team guys.

They stuffed us into the Boxes as soon as we got to the Interrogation Center. Now these damn things where just big enough for a normal man to lay in a tight Fetal position. If you were exceptionally limber you could turn over, with a lot of work and pain. I was in the Box just over Commander Ryan. He told me later that the Instructors (Guards), became extremely pissed off, when I fell asleep and started snoring. Their remedy was using their night sticks to beat on the side of the boxes, every once in a while, in a vain attempt to keep me awake. If they weren't beating, I was sleeping.

The five of us where in the Boxes for about thirty minutes, when they started bringing in more of our classmates. Before we were returned to the main compound, I made two mistakes, that Mister by the Book, Irish Ryan, would let me hear about. The first was a little classmate abuse, I would happily do again, Commander Ryan or no. The second, was just pure, not thinking things out.

After about forty-minutes, they took me out of my Box, and put me in a Box with another guy. This Box was half again as large as the normal Box, and with two guys, a damn tight fit. Since we hadn't had changed our clothes, or showered in a few days, the smell was not pleasant. Truthfully, this didn't bother me all that much.

What got to me was, he was a screamer; the asshole, just would not shut up.

I even tried being mister nice guy, first. When that didn't work, you might say, I took matters into my own hands: It took me about another twenty-minutes or so, to put and end to it. In the double box, it was damn near impossible to move anything, but the tips of your fingers and toes. With a lot of pain I worked my hand into his crotch, and grasped my classmate by his balls.

He didn't get a loving caress, and in the short term, my action caused the opposite effect of what I desired. He screamed louder then ever, but when I let up compressing his balls, to about half there normal size, he quit screaming and started crying. I then informed the asshole, that if he didn't shut up, I would rip his fucking NUTS off. Since his family jewels were in my firm grip, he took me serious, and shut the fuck up.

I was only in the Double Box, another fifteen minutes, after my classmate quit screaming. He had calmed down to a soft whimper, and I just started to doze off, when our Instructors, removed us from the Box. Our fake Commies, were treating the asshole I had abused, as if he were their long lost, injured brother.

Two Instructors, were helping him walk around the room, getting the kinks out of his muscles. They even asked if he wanted some water, or would he like to sit down. I knew the whiny shit head would sign some kind of War Crime statement. What got me chewed out by

Commander Ryan, was how they got him to sign. I had been taken out of the Interrogation Center, and over to the Red Cross Center. Irish was laying in his box, not ten feet away, when they told the shit head, what they would do to him, if he didn't sign a statement.

They had discovered a weak link, and had used me to soften him up for the kill. The Screamer was told that I was crazy, and they were sorry, but if he didn't cooperate, they would put him back in the BOX, with me. The rest of the guys told me later that he had started crying like a baby, not just whimpering, but bawling. I would find out what they did with those kind of guys, shortly after my next screw up at the at the Red Cross Center.

The Red Cross building was only about thirty feet from the Interrogation Center, but was worlds apart in how you were treated. "The Rules of War", say the Red Cross must have access to all war time prison camps and prisoners. Yeah right, rules of war. At the Red Cross Center you, were informed of your rights. They asked you to give them your family's address, so they could let them know you were all right. The Red Cross worker had me setting in a nice comfortable chair, sipping coffee, and eating a cookie. He had me by the balls, just as surely as I had my classmates in my hand, in the Double Box.

After our nice little chat, I was sent to another room for a physical by a Red Cross Doctor. Well that's where they got a picture of me, with my right hand in the air, and a Communist Flag behind me. I appeared to be swearing allegiance to something or other. The good Doctor had been giving me a physical, he told me he was checking my coordination and reflexes. It went something like this; close your eyes, raise your right foot, raise your left hand, head high, put down your right foot, pick up your left foot, put down your left hand, raise your right hand, head high, put down your left foot, open your eyes. When I opened my eyes a bright flash went off. The good Doctor turned out to be, not so good after all.

They were teaching us, what many of our POW's in Korea had learned the hard way, THE COMMIES DID NOT PLAY BY THE RULES. It was a simple thing, but it sure made me feel stupid. A very clear Polaroid picture of me standing in front of a Commie Flag, with my right hand raised, like I was swearing allegiance.

You might ask, so what? When they have you for the long hall, they have time to mess with your mind. They could make up a dummy Home town paper, with that picture on the front page, or just circulate the picture among your fellow prisoners. Anything to cause trouble between the prisoners. If the other prisoners turn on you, you are either dead, or become a Commie.

Our phony commies where about to make a little mistake, witch of course, I jumped on, "like stink on a skunk." There are just two types of escape, from any type of incarceration.

#1. Planed: An escape thought out, and set up, over a period of time.

#2. Opportunity: These happen now, on the spur of the moment. You have to recognize the opportunity and act. The prisoner must always be looking for momentary lapses in the system. Planed escape was what Commander Ryan had set up. Not fifteen minutes after they snapped the picture of me, I had an escape of opportunity, or so I thought.

After my phony Red Cross interview, I had been escorted to the outer compound gate, by one Guard. He opened the gate, pointed to the gate between the inner and outer compounds, and told me to report to the Guard on the inner Compound Gate.

As he shut the Outer Compound Gate, the Guard on the Inner Gate walked away from his post, further into the Inner Compound. I quickly glanced back over my shoulder, the Guard that had walked me to the Outer Gate, had his back to me. A glance up, and to my right, at the Guard Tower over looking the Outer Compound. I couldn't see the Guard, he was either on the far side of the Tower, or screwing off. I made my move.

In the middle of the Outer Compound, was a clapboard building, about fifteen by twenty feet, supported on cement blocks. The building had a space, about fifteen to sixteen inches, between the ground and its floor. I hauled ass, across the fifty or so feet between me and the building, and made a dive for the dark space under it.

My education, as to the human condition, was about to move to the Graduate Studies level. For the next hour, I laid under the floor of that clap board building, and listened to cowards. Young men who were giving up their country, and classmates over this piss-ant little bit of pressure, a stupid little game. When I first arrived under the building, it was empty. For the first five minutes I laid very still, waiting, not a sound through the wood floor above, no one came after me. Now how in the Hell do I get the rest of the way out of the camp?

I crawled to the West side of the building, where I could get a good look at the Watch Tower and outer fence along that side of the compound. I must have laid there another ten minutes, trying to figure out how to get the rest of the way out of the camp. I had put myself in a box.

No one knew where I was, the one dark spot in the middle of the well lit outer compound. To make good my escape, I would have to cross another fifty feet of clear well lit dirt. Go over or under the eighteen foot fence. All in plain view of all four watch towers, and most of the main compound.

I was laying there concluding I was not in a good spot, when any interest in even attempting the rest of my escape, went out of my head. The room I was laying under, was the Indoctrination Center, a school house for quitters. They brought about ten of my classmates, out of the inter-compound gate, and across to the room I lay under. My Graduate Studies were on.

Before we turned ourselves in, Commander Ryan and I had observed them bringing small groups of prisoners over to the little building that I lay under. We had known a little about what was thought to go on in there, from Team members who had been through the school. We hadn't been able to find one Team member that had been taken to that shed. Irish figured they only took people in there they thought might sign an anti-American statement, or confess to a War Crime. We had been told that several guys from each class would do this. My escape of " Opportunity" quickly became, "Human Nature 101" and a great source of food.

I could hear them being read selections from Communist material written by Karl Marks and Chairman Mao. They would be asked questions about the meaning of what was just read, and if someone gave them the answer they were looking for, they got a cookie. Two of that first group signed War Crimes confessions; admitting to killing children and raping women. Their reward was nothing more then a sandwich, some fruit and a couple cookies. When they took them back to the main compound, our heroes read their confessions, in front of God and everybody, over the camp P. A. system.

As soon as they had taken them all back to the main compound, I had slipped from under the shed and inside. The first thing that caught my eye, was a shelf about three feet off the floor, with sandwiches, fruit and little packs of cookies stacked on it. On the floor, up against three walls where open G-11-A parachute canopies.

The damn things are a 110 foot in diameter; they're used to drop tanks and other heavy loads. They made nice cushy seats for our Commie collaborators. From where they sat, the food on the shelf was at eye level. Screw it, I took two sandwiches, a pair, two packs of cookies, and got back under the shed.

Right after our cowardly classmates read their confessions, the Guards figured out yours truly was missing. You might say " The Kaka had hit the propeller". They had lined everyone in the main compound up, counted the guys at the Interrogation Center, and come up one man short, me. They would be running around in the hinterland for the rest of the night, looking for what they assumed to be, their injured student. Oh well, to quote some sailor from back in pre-history " Fuck'em if they can't take a joke".

Laying under that little building, listening for the rest of the night, would occupy a good part of my thought process for several years to come. The only history I knew was what I had lived through, and the Korean War was part of that. My Dad had fought in the Second World War II, my Uncle in Korea. I knew our little play prisoner of war camp was nothing compared to the real thing.

THE TERRORIST

That night, laying under the S.E.A.R. Indoctrination Center, the question of why took over my mind. I just couldn't understand how so many grown men, had given up so easy. I mean hell, even then I knew any of us could be broken, myself included. But these assholes were willing to sell themselves and their country after a few days of being a little hungry. The truth is, it was damn hard not to come from under the shed and slap the crap out of the weak willed bastards myself.

Around dawn, the group that had been above my head for the last hour was moved back to the compound. It was time to turn myself in, I could smell Oatmeal being cooked. Our short time as communist prisoner would come to end with a hot breakfast. I crawled out from under the shed, and walked to the Inter-compound gate. I stood by the gate for a couple of minutes before anyone paid any attention to me. Then a ton of SHIT hit the Fan for me.

As the Head of Instructor approached the gate, I hollered Hey Comrade let me in. Wow the Comrades lost it , the gate was flung open, and a whole pack of 'em where on me. They where all around me, shouting, three or four of them pulling and slapping. With that I lost it. The head instructor was right in front of me slapping and screaming, fuck'em, I caught him with a short little uppercut.

My little uppercut caused three things to happen in short order;

1) The Head Instructor tongue was bitten through as his jaw slammed shut.

2) He dropped to his knees.

3) The rest of our Commie Instructors piled on yours truly, some of them doing a little punching of their own.

Now the next minute or so was nothing less then an old fashioned punch out. They had the numbers, but had to aim their punches. I just had to stay on my feet, keep my head covered and kick any shin I could. I if you have never experienced a good kick in the shin ask someone to do it; it will quickly change your thought process, from whatever you were doing, to focusing on the sudden and intense pain in your lower extremity.

I don't really know how long it lasted, but about the time a couple of the Instructors got smart, and started working on my exposed ribs, my Teammates started breaking it up. I could hear Commander Ryan's voice booming ADMINISTRATIVE, ADMINISTRATIVE.

The next thing I remember I'm on my knees, finding it very painful to breath . The Head Commie is being helped to his feet, with a lot of blood dripping from his mouth. You might say breakfast was off for me. Even with the pain of what felt like broken ribs, making it hurt to breath, I knew I might damn well be looking at Portsmouth Naval Prison and a Bad Conduct Discharge.

The deal was, I had smacked a United Navy Master

Chief with a good uppercut, a very big no-no in the Navy. The Chief was standing over me, screaming with blood flying in every direction. His ranting boiled down he was going to see I lost my Secret Clearance, was Court Marshaled, and thrown out of the Navy. All six foot four inches of Commander Ryan stepped between the Chief and me and boomed out in a very commanding voice, "Shut up Chief, or you and your school will receive a Fitness Report you won't believe". Not only the Chief, but everyone shut up.

Irish proceeded to tell the head Instructor that I had not broken the school rules, I had never left the compound, and where I had been. He personally had observed me moving from under the Indoctrination shed, to inside and back out three times during the night. He ordered the Instructors to have the Chief and me checked out by the school medical staff. There was to be no further discussion about what had just transpired.

In many ways it was my lucky day. No charges where placed against me for smacking the Chief, and all I ended up with was three cracked, not broken ribs. When the Navy Doctor was done checking me out Commander Ryan assured me that I would not have any problems stemming from the little punch out with the fake Commies. He and the Commanding Officer of the school had come to an agreement: No charges on me, none on them.

I did get a mild ass chewing over my actions in the

double box. Lt. Commander Ryan reminded me that I had not helped my screaming classmate, as ordered, but instead my actions had helped push him over the edge. He also let me know that the picture of me, standing in front of a Commie Flag with my hand raised like I was swearing allegiance, would hang in his Office. Irish Ryan said just one more thing to me, and it blew my socks off. He put his big hand on my shoulder, gave me a rare big Irish smile, and said "Good fucking job Austin!"

JUNGLE ENVIRONMENTAL SURVIVAL TRAINING or (JEST) was run by the Negrito's, the earliest known inhabitants of the Philippine Islands. The first time I saw the Negrito's was in 1960, as a seventeen year old on one of my first overseas liberties. I had come across two children over a hundred feet up in a tree near the old Subic Bay Naval Exchange. Hell I had been one of those children that climbed tall trees, but these little kids were scaring the crap out of me.

As it turned out they weren't children, they were very small men. When they came down from the tree, I had gone over to see what it was the had wrapped in their loin clothes. It was bird eggs, they had been gathering dinner. These guys were naked except for a small loin cloth, and maybe four foot and a few inches tall. They were well muscled, dark brown and moved with confident grace. Each had a spear taller than me, six foot one, and a knife that hung to there knees. One thing struck me right off the bat, these people didn't feel out of place. Believe me they had my attention, over the next few years, I would learn a lot from, and about these people.

In the area of Subic Bay Naval Station, there were two tribes of Negrito's. In the 60s, besides running the JEST school, both tribes were contracted to guard the perimeters of the base that ran through the jungle. Their pay, dump rights, they could have any damn thing the United States Navy threw away. Keep in mind this was in the days before recycling, and things that would be re-used today were just thrown away. That first trip to Subic Bay I had witnessed why no one messed with the Negrito's

It seemed that jet parts were disappearing from a hanger on the Naval Air Station. Base Security couldn't figure out who was doing the steeling, so the Negrito's came under suspicion. Now the Tribes were not responsible for any security, other then the base fences that ran through the jungles surrounding at least three quarters of the base. Well when the tribes had come under suspicion, the Negrito's took matters into their own hands.

They quickly caught two Filipino civilian employees of the base steeling parts. The thieves where hung, half dead, from the top of the 12 foot fence near the base main gate. Then the Negrito's did the most amazing thing; The tribes had surrounded the area, armed only with their spears, knifes, and bows and would not let anyone take the two thieves down until they had died.

Both fully armed U.S. Marines and the local Filipino Police had approached the Negrito's, trying to get the thieves down. Each time the Negrito's had gotten ready to do battle, the police, then the Marines had backed off. The two thieves had hung there for a day and half, in full view of the inhabitants of Olongapo City. When they had finally died, the Negrito Tribesmen had left them hang on the fence, and walked back into their jungle. A little quick justice, that gave the Negrito people a place in my heart, forever.

My first up close up and personal contact with Negrito's was a half day in the classroom and three and half days in the jungle. For me it would become more then the no-stop training the Teams were always involved in. It would be the first of seven trips I made into the jungles of the Philippines, with those little masters of the survival and mayhem, two with my platoon and five with just me, Master Chief Jimmy Henily and one amazing little Negrito friend.

That first trip, fourteen U. S. Navy Frogmen and two Negrito's walked into the jungle with the clothes on our back, a Bola Knife and a bag of salt. We had on jungle style camouflage jackets and trousers, with jungle boots on our feet. The Negrito's wore nothing but a loin cloth. We ate like kings, slept comfortable, and generally just had a full on three and a half day learning experience.

By the forth night were camped less then 150 yards from the 18th green on the naval base golf course. The only way you could tell you weren't in the deepest part of the darkest jungle in the world, was the sound of jets taking off and landing at the naval base. We had trekked through the Philippine Jungle 6 hours each day, moving as a combat patrol. Each time our Negrito Instructors wanted to teach us something, we stopped and had a mini class. Most of the time they would have us gather plants and herbs, then move on.

Each night they had a pre-picked camp site where practical classes would continue for another four or so hours. We learned things like: what plants to eat, which to use for medicine, how to capture fish by hand, make a pressure cooker from Giant Bamboo, how to make sleeping platforms and quick shelters to keep the rain off.

The main thing I learned was, compared to Negrito's, we were babies in the jungle. Just watching them move through the dense growth was a lesson onto itself: Now you see 'em, now you don't. They might just blend into the jungle 20 feet up ahead of you and then, silently appear at your side.

Our last camp was on the side of a hill over looking a beautiful little waterfall that cascaded into a crystal clear pond about a hundred yards long and maybe twenty wide. There was a big old mango tree, with a rope on a limb that grew out over the pond. Of course a bunch of SEALs took complete advantage of that nice size body of beautiful water and the two cases of San Miguel beer cooling at the bottom. Anyone looking on would never believe that this tranquil scene was the geneses of the Terrorist. The tranquility part took place after Henily and I had whipped all comers in a little two on two "Slaughter Ball Water Polo".

It's a pretty simple game; You find something to simulate a ball, in this case, an inflated demolition flotation bladder. There is just one rule, the winner gets the ball to the opponents end of what ever body of water you have at hand.

As in any battle those with the most guile that know when to properly apply violence, come out on top. Any non-Team member watching the game would have figured we hated each other, not the case! We in fact loved each other enough to demand huge effort to win.

That evening as Master Chief Jimmy Henily and I sat on the hill overlooking that jungle pond, nursing our wounds, drinking beer and talking, the inception of The Terrorist took place. That first trip into the Philippine Jungle, had brought together a chain of questions in my mind: Why had those guys admitted committing war crimes the night I lay under the Indoctrination Building at S.E.R.E. School?

I mean hell, why are some people so strong and others so weak? What makes strong people? Why do we in the United States have it so good? Believe me friends, poor people in our country have more monetary wealth, then a whole village of Negrito people. Most of all, why in the hell, didn't we appreciate what we have?

THE TERRORIST

After listening to me spout senseless answers to my own questions for a couple hours, Chief said "Get your head out of your ass Austin, study some fucking history, just maybe you'll understand why, what you just said is a load of shit!" I had just made some comment about, if the Government would just do such and such everything would be all right, when the Chief had dumped on me.

One of the things that struck me odd about my Chief was, I knew him to be a PATRIOTS PATRIOT but he didn't like the Government much. I would spend every free minute of the next few years before I got out of the Teams, doing as Master Chief Jimmy Henily had suggested, studying World and U. S. History. Then I would understand.

Just like walking out of that theater, after seeing the Frogmen, I knew my life had changed. I didn't know how yet, but sitting with Master Chief Henily over looking that jungle pool, I was sure my life had just taken a new turn. The chain of my life runs true, from that moment to this. Sorry Master Chief but my reading of history is a little different then yours.

I would spend a good part of the next four years killing people I had nothing against. As we all know, it hasn't been much problem killing people that I figured had it coming. I knew I would never kill again just because someone pissed me off, al-la First Class Gunners Mates Gary D. Fine. I was still bothered by my murder of Fine, as I am to this day. Combat

Combat boils down to this: It ain't Nice! I think it was said best by one of my Teammates "It is this simple, if they are willing to kill people and break things, and you are not, they win. One ugly fact about human nature is: If someone will not fight for what is theirs, they lose it". I'll tell you about on my first and last combat experience. It may help you understand my thoughts on living and dieing.

We all knew combat was close at hand. A few Team guys had already been to the Nam. Most people who didn't fight there call it Vietnam. It was an odd war, run from the White House not the Pentagon. We lost no battles, our troops kicked ass, yet we lost the war. For those of us that fought there, it will always be the Nam, everywhere else was known as The World.

Oddly enough my first combat kills came in the Philippines, not in Nam. From my days in UDT till I left SEAL Team, we where always involved with the Plumbers, Spooks, CIA whatever you chose to call them. These where known as "Black Operations". Meaning they where never to see the light of day. The Who, What and Why, where never to be known. It was a level of Team Op's that not all Team members where involved in.

In those days the main bad guys in the Philippines where called the Huks. They called themselves Communist but never put up much of a front of helping the small guy. They where into every racket you could imagine: drugs, gun running, black market cigarettes, prostitution, murder for hire, you name it they did it.

The top of the heap Huks where all rich guys using the phony Commie label to make themselves richer. Well they fucked up big time. One of the Huks leaders had a wife and six of a Negrito Chief children slaughtered. It was intended as a message, the Chief wouldn't allow his tribal area to be used for smuggling. The Huks thought they would teach him a lesson. Well my friends they where in for a big nasty surprise.

It had taken about a week and every one of the Huks that had done the killing was found near death. They where staked out spread-eagle, near a major highway intersection, with their guts hanging out. The Negrito's had not damaged any organs, they had even made neat slices in their in the lower stomach.

All these guys would have lived except for one other little thing. Their stomach cavities had been filled with Bat Shit. These assholes where going to have a long, slow and painful death from infection. The Negrito's wanted everyone to know who had done the deed and why it was done. The whole tribe had stood near the staked out murders until the police and an army unit had showed up. They then just melted back into the jungle and of course no one followed.

This particular Chief had been the wrong man to mess with. His tribe had been particularly helpful to us during World War 11. As a young man he had killed more Japanese then could be counted. When our, or the Filipino Government, needed to deal with the Negrito's they went through this Chief and him alone. All the tribes where very independent and wanted little to do with any government and not much with each other. This Chief was trusted to not give anything away and keep the government off their asses.

I had just finished running a Jump School, at Fort Mecsisi, for the Philippine Navy Underwater Demolition Unit, UDU. We worked closely with all our allied countries Frogmen. There was a big party planned for that evening and I had been looking forward to it. Oh well, the Commanding Officer of UDU, called me aside, it seemed someone had other plans: "You are ordered to head for Subic Bay. Be at the Pang Wa Halfway House no later then 21:00 hours, you will be met and receive orders from someone you know. As far as anyone is concerned, you must join your platoon for an imminent operation."

You might ask why I would take orders from a foreign Naval Officer? I had been assigned, TAD (Temporary Additional Duty) to his Command. Something not that unusual in any military, amongst allies. What was unusual, was how the orders where given: In private, verbal with no specifics. It could mean only one thing, Spooks/CIA.

I had about three hours to get to the Pang Wa Halfway House, only thirty some miles toward Subic Bay. These miles being on the highways of the Philippines, I got my ass on the road in a hurry.

THE TERRORIST

In those days the roads in the PI where not much. In the rainy season bridges where washed out on a regular basis. There where large trucks on small, badly maintained, two lane highways. When they got into an accident, everything stopped. The Philippines are not one island but hundred's. They are mountain tops, covered in jungle, jutting up from the sea. Ninety present of the country is up and down, not an easy place to get around.

Let me tell ya, my adrenaline was flowing, I had to stop twice and do a few sets of push-up alongside the road. If this was real deal Spook shit, I had to have tight control of myself when I got to Pang Wa. It took me almost the whole trip to get my brain slowed down and the self-control I needed. When I pulled off the two lane highway, and around back of the Pang Wa Halfway House, I was about twenty minutes early. Low and behold who stepped out of the Jungle but Master Chief Jimmy Henily.

He gave me the hand-signal to follow him and stepped back into the jungle. Thank God for small favors, was my thought as I followed Henily into the jungle. If he was on this Operation, all I had to do was take my cues from him and I couldn't go wrong.

About twenty yards into the jungle was a clearing that Henily and I stopped in. Waiting for us was a Team member of ours. He and I where about the same size, both of us with blond hair and blue eyes.

Our Teammates part on this operation was cover for me. We swapped clothes, he went into the halfway house, ate, had a beer and drove the jeep back to Subic Bay. I had gone from civilian clothes to improvised jungle gear.

Nothing new or made in the USA. My Dog Tags and Military ID had gone with my civilian clothes, back to Subic. I was armed with a Chinese combat knife, a Chinese knock off of the Russian AK-47, and six French Hand Grenades. Henily was outfitted the same way but carried a French made PP-11 radio. The Chinese Communist had a lot of French made equipment.

I wasn't carrying or wearing anything a good Chinese Communist might not have. All I was told is: "This is not training, we are on a clandestine operation!" For the next two hours we used evasive tactics, good sneak and peak technique, ending up at another jungle clearing. Knowing we had not been followed, at least that is what I thought.

We had approached the clearing as if it was being held by the bad guys. Henily had been doing radio checks at fifteen minutes intervals. These where done by keying the radio, no voice. Every time you key the radio, it makes a click sound, so many click at such and such time, means a certain thing.

No voice communication between us, all our communication where done by hand signals. After we had crawled to the edge of the clearing and observed it for several minutes, Henily coughed once, it was quickly answered with two coughs. The Chief signaled me, "Himself, and three people."

Since we had left the clearing behind the halfway house I had been told nothing more about the operation. As my Chief stepped into the clearing my mind set was: Cover his back, one odd move and everyone else dies. Two Filipinos and one Negrito stepped into the clearing at the same time Chief Henily did. Each coming into the clearing from a different area of jungle. I was damn sure I was not the only eyes watching from the perimeter of the clearing. What would surprise me is just how many set of eyes.

For any Black Op to be pulled off, many parts have to operate perfectly. The thing is most of those parts, not only don't know what the other parts are doing, they don't even know what the other parts are. Now if this Op would have gone as planed my first combat kills would have come in Nam not in the PI. The truth is most of my kills while in the military came because an Op didn't go as planed. This one sure didn't.

One of the Filipino's was an American spook; the other was a member of Philippine Navy Underwater Demolition Unit. Better known as UDU, their Frogmen. I didn't recognize the Negrito but I would find out years later he was the only surviving child of the Chief whose family had been slaughtered.

After about ten minutes, Henily signaled me in. As I came in, one other American and one other Filipino UDU member, stepped into clearing as well. What I didn't see until we left the clearing, was the twenty or so, Negrito Warriors surrounding the clearing as our security.

I'll try to make this as clear as possible, without using a bunch of bla bla military terms. We were briefed on the Operation in the clearing. It boiled down to this, the Philippine and our Governments wanted the Negrito Chief to get his revenge, with as little problem as possible. The Negrito's had extracted, who had given the order, from the Huks found along the highway.

The head Huk was from a very rich and politically well connected family. He lived in a heavily guarded compound in Manila. The basic problem was, to get him out of there and into the hands of the Negrito Chief, with out much commotion. The Negrito's are the best I've ever seen at blending into the jungle! In a city they stand out like a Nun in a strip joint.

The Chief, the Spook and I where to be the back up for the two Filipino Frogmen. There part was to lure Mister Big into a trap. Both had been doing a little undercover work for the Philippine Government. They had been selling larger and larger quantities of American made cigarettes and ammunition on the black-market. Both governments had been gathering intelligence on the Huks and their grip on organized crime for a couple years.

THE TERRORIST

The slaughter of the Chiefs wife and children had given them a way, to get rid of a big problem, without having to prosecute. In the PI, if you where well connected, it was almost impossible to prosecute you. The whole legal system ran on: Who you know or what you can pay. The well connected Mr. Big Huk, would be damn near impossible to convict in a court of law. So our governments had hatched a plan to see that a little jungle justice, was done.

It was suppose to work like this. The top Huks son had been buying large quantities of ammunition from the two undercover Filipino Frogman. In all the deals they had done with him, he had found a way to rip them off to one degree or another. The plan was, on the up coming deal, they where going to take the son hostage. Junior was to be held till the missing money from deals already done were paid. At least that's what his dad had to believe.

The plan called for the son to be snatched during the next ammo delivery to a small island just outside Manila Harbor. The swap, money for son, would be done on a boat in Manila Harbor. The last place the Big Huk would be worried about the jungle dwellers. Of course our plan was that both father and son would end up in the hands of the very ticked off Negrito Chief.

Now I know most of you have heard of the Six P's, "Prior Planning Prevents Piss Poor Performance." Well it does, but not in the way most people think. It's like this, NOTHING GOES BY THE PLAN. What good planing does is make it apparent that things are not going well before it's too late to react to the problem. Great planing is about who does what when the plan turns to SHIT.

Where our plan started to smell like fertilizer was in taking the son, he had his own double cross in mind. His plan had been to kill both the Filipino Frogmen, take the ammunition and pocket the money. As it turned out, the double cross would give me my first combat kills and bring home the importance of good planing. I have a little saying I made up while in Training for the Teams. "Paranoia is healthy, after all, we are dealing with humans here." It differently applied here!

Jim and I had been inserted, along with the American Filipino Spook, on a small island in Manila Bay, four days before the Ammo delivery was to take place. The Spook had one highly paid informant on the island, a very pissed off Filipino fisherman whose only daughter had been used rather rudely by the big Huks son and his men.

To add insult to injury the son had given the father about 10 dollars worth of Pesos for his daughter's virginity. Our informer had no idea what his information and hand drawn maps where for. The three of us had talked it over and come to the decision that the less the informant knew the better. Hell he had already switched sides once.

In many ways he could have been helpful to have someone on the inside. The island was under daddy's complete control, the local fisherman all sold their fish to a fishery he owned. They received prime price for their fish and extra when they brought in a smuggled load of ammo, cigarettes, drugs, whatever he was dealing in at the time. You might say we were fixing to snatch the son in his own backyard.

It was essentially a combat insertion. We had come ashore in a French Inflatable boat, launched from a fishing vessel a mile off the island, at 01:00. We had planed the insertion so the current was in our favor. God Bless my Chief, Jimmy had played it close and tight and it's a damn good thing he did.

Our first order of business had been sinking the boat, cover our tracks and find three good spots to hole up. By 04:30 each of us was on a separate hill overlooking the compound, the Huks used when doing business on the island. That way we couldn't be taken as a group while we slept. While two of us caught some Zeees, the third man kept watch from a distance.

We had carried no equipment that a good Chinese Communist wouldn't have. Yes even in those days the French dealt with anyone behind their supposed allies back, that's why we used a Zodiac boat and their very good French radio the PP-11. We weren't on the island six hours and our plan had turned to fertilizer. The plan had been to find three places to hide, during daylight hours, and do our major recons over the next couple nights. We would then make our plan and carry it out

We had inserted four days before the meeting to do a little, Sneak and Peak, around the island and get ourselves set up. The son and his crew usually showed up a couple days early. They liked to have a little fun away from prying eyes.

As it was, we didn't get two days, they had shown up not six hours after we hit the island. We where out numbered eight to three, the son and a seven man fire team. Not the four he had with him on his previous dealings with our two Filipino Frogmen friends. It was readily apparent, they where up to, a little extra No Good and the smell of our plan was decidedly shitty.

They had spent the morning getting their gear moved into their compound, while we watched from our hills above. Several of the local women had spent most of the afternoon preparing for the nights activities. That first night while the Huks had what I could only call a Pig Roast/Orgy, we found out why they had arrived two days early.

The three of us had spent the early evening Sneaking and Peeking off our individual hills. We rendezvoused in the jungle a 100 meters behind the Huks compound. We talked over options and Master Chief Henily decided first we would: Recon the perimeter of the compound, if possible penetrate it, with No Contact.

For you that have never been in the military, that means just what it says . Do not let anyone see, hear or even smell you. We where to gather all the intelligence we could in four hours and meet a hundred meters to the south of our current position.

Henily backed tracked and took up a good shooting position on the closest hill overlooking the village. Jimmy was giving us cover encase we screwed up. He would throw down as much distracting fire as he could if we where in trouble. We had several "What If's" set up, where to go and what to do if so and so happened.

Our Spook friend and I stashed all our weapons, except our knifes, touched up our camouflage and started the long slow crawl to the Compound perimeter. You might ask why we went so lightly armed. Well this was meant to be a No Contact Recon, try crawling with an AK-47 and Ammo, it's just not very quiet.

The party had been in full swing as we crawled toward the compound. You could smell the roasting pig and hear the music and laughter. These guys belonged dead, what a bunch of assholes. We could of crawled right into the camp and killed every damn one of them with just our knives. They where all eating and drinking, in different stages of undress and sexual activity.

No security posted, all of them were partying hardy, well on the way to being dead drunk. Their boat had even been left on guarded, tied to a small pier south of the main village. We not only Re-coned from their perimeter, we spent over two hours sneaking and peaking all over their compound. By the time we crawled out of the Huks camp half of them where passed out.

When we reached our rendezvoused point with Jimmy, I was sure the compound was ours for the taking. We now knew why they had come early. Our Spook had not been ten feet from the Big Huks son, while he bragged on how he would personally kill the two UDU Frogman. It was all about money, he hadn't found out they where undercover. The greedy bastard just wanted the Ammo and to put his dads money in his own pocket.

Henily had listened to us both and ask several questions. We then hatched our plan, what you might call a Slaughter of Opportunity. Jimmy made it clear, object number one, was getting the Big Huks son out of there in one piece and making sure dad thought the gun running Frogmen had him for Ransom.

The rest of the Op would be done at a Crash and Burn pace. Before we entered the compound I had made sure I could quickly hot-wire the Huks boat. Everyman in the compound but the son, would be killed. Our Filipino Spook crawled into the compound first.

His job was to get the one women still in compound out of there without disturbing our passed out Huks. She would be the key to selling our: Holding your son for ransom fiction. It took our Spook all of ten minutes to have her, gagged, bound and out of the compound in the tree line. He spent another five minutes speaking to her in, Tagalla a dialect of the Filipino language.

She was told to tell the Big Huk that if he wanted his Son returned he had to pay what he owed us and then some. She had only seen our Filipino Spook and been spoken to in her own language. The Big Huk would have to think it was the Filipino Frogman that had his son.

The rest was almost to easy, not what you would call a fair fight. We had quietly moved back into the compound, gagged and bound the son, before he could make a sound. Then went about the bad business of slitting seven passed out mens throats. As with nearly all people that die a violent death, most of them had shit their pants as they died.

I picked the Big Huks son up, draped him over my shoulder and headed for our boat. The rest for Chief Henily and I was over quickly. We hot wired the boat, broke radio silence and let our contact know: The What, the Where and the Why. We had pulled of the objective, the trouble was it was, not by the plan or the time frame.

Now it was up to our support team to react and do it quick. An hour later we rendezvoused with two boats. Chief Henily and I went one way, the Filipino Spook and the Huks son another. In all Black Ops, once your part is done, you are told nothing. It is called Need to Know and is one way information is kept from leaking out.

I would have never known the outcome of my first Black Op, except that some years later, I spent time in the PI jungles, with the Negrito tribe involved: Yes the Big Huk and his son where turned over to the Negrito Chief. The Negrito Chief had the Big Huk and his son staked out in the middle of his jungle village. They where given just enough water and food to keep them from dieing to quickly.

Now this might not sound overly cruel but think about this: They where spread eagle, never allowed to move, as they wasted away in your own shit and piss. The Negrito's just went about their daily business as the little bugs and critters of the jungle used the Big Huk and his son as a Free Lunch Wagon. I like to think of it as the Big Huk and his son became: Just Dessert for the bugs.

THE TERRORIST

My Last Nam Shoot'em Up

I did my last combat operation in the Navy four years after we snatched the Big Huks son. In those four years about two and a half had been spent in the Nam. Most of the Army and Marines where doing a year in country and then home never to return. Of course being Team guys we did it a little differently: In general we would spend six months in country and six out.

That is when you where in an operating platoon, fourteen men, seven in each Fire Team. There where all kinds of little side trips that could last from one day to three months, in most cases those where Black Ops. Some like Phoenix and the PRU Program have become public knowledge but many have never seen the light of day and remain Black. During that time I had read over forty books on American History. I had formulated my plan to become The Terrorist and by the time my last Team Op came around had laid the basic ground work. In fact I couldn't wait to get started.

My last Op was with a Operating Platoon but it wasn't mine, it wasn't even my Team. In those days, there where only two SEAL Teams, SEAL Team 1 on the West Coast and SEAL Team 2 on the East Coast, I was a member of Team 1. Both SEAL Teams and all five of the UDTs, 21 and 22 East Coast and 11,12 &13 West Coast, operated in the Nam. We where spread all over the damn place doing all kinds of crazy shit.

Chief Henily and I had been in country for about two weeks doing a simple in and out problem solving. We had eliminated, murdered, a Vietnamese Government Official, who was a spy for the North Vietnamese. It had only taken about two minutes to do the job, all the rest of the time was spent setting it up so it looked like a random crime. We had just completed the Op and gotten back to Da Nang when I received new Orders.

On a personal level this was one of those ."So you want to be a frogman" moments! My Brother Jim and the Chiefs daughter, Judith Jo where getting married. They had scheduled the wedding believing yours truly could attend. Boats and I where to be dual Best Men, something I was really looking forward to. It comes down to this for the Teams: If you're going to be a warrior, being a warrior comes first. An old Navy Chief summed it up the best I ever heard! " The Navy didn't issue you that family with your sea-bag!" Cold but true!

Detachment "Alpha" Bravo Platoon, SEAL Team 2 was down in Cantoe and needed a Radio Man, one of theirs had been hit. They would be finishing up in three week and heading home about the time I was due to get out. Little did I know that the Pucker Factor was soon to be the most intense, of my young but exciting life! For those who don't understand Pucker Factor: When your Ass is so tight there is no hole. That my friend is a pucker factor of 10!

I knew most of the guys in Det "Alpha" and my old Classmate, Shorty Flacktum, was acting Senior Petty

Officer. The Platoon Chief and a Radioman had been shot up pretty bad in a Firefight, that none of then should have walked out of. They had engaged a Company of North Vietnamese Regulars about ready to finish off a 4 man Army LURPS Patrol, all Army Rangers.

Back in those days when Special Operation for all services where not well understood or financed and often misused: There was a lot of: You watch my my back and I'll watch yours. The Army had some Rangers running Long Range Reconnaissance Patrols, commonly known as LURPS around the Canto area. There basic missions generally ran along the lines of : We think the enemy might over here, go out there and find out what you can.

The Rangers problem like ours in the Teams could be boiled down to: People giving them orders who had no idea what a Ranger should be doing anyway. So the senior Non-commissioned Officers; Chiefs, Master & Gunnery Sergeants of the Navy, Army and Marine Corps made sure they backed each other action. Senior Noncoms would attend each other's Warning Orders and respond to any, before, during or after call for help they could.

A good part of the Teams, bad-assed, reputation in the Nam came from a couple of the support groups we had watching our backs. Navy Seawolves and The Riverine Forces. The Seawolf's flew the Huey Helicopters with 14 rockets and six M-60 Machine Guns, commonly called gunships. The Riverine Forces were known as the

Brown Water Navy. These sailors main vessel was the PBR (Patrol Boat River) but they had everything from LSTs to heavily armed Mike 8 Landing Craft.

Just like the Teams, Seawolf's and Riverine, where all Navy volunteers. The point of these guys was not the weapons: It was, if we needed them they where their! No questions ask, not time wasted getting some a-hole to clear their Operation. No one else I know of in the Nam had that kind of support. They would lie, steal and cheat to get us in and out in one piece.

When the Rangers call for help had come, both fire teams, all 14 members of Detachment "Alpha" Bravo Platoon, SEAL Team 2, saddled up in four Huey Seawolf Gunships. Keep in mind four, United States Army Rangers, where surrounded and holding off at least a full Company of North Vietnamese Regulars, somewhere around 150 + enemy troops.

Three of the four Rangers had already taken hits, wounded but all were still fighting. They were surrounded about a click, a thousand meters from the river. Det. "Alpha's" Platoon Officer called for PPR support as they where lifting off in the Seawolf's. He and the Seawolf's Commanding Officer had a rough plan: Have the Rangers pull smoke to identify their position. All four Seawolf's would hit the enemy from North, South, East and West of the smoke, Rockets and M-60.

When they had spread a little confusion amongst the

enemy, each gunship would take turns getting their SEALs on the ground with the Rangers. The other three gunships, would be giving the one offloading helicopter, cover. It was going to take the PBR's another 45 minutes to an hour to be in position for the extraction along the river bank. Everyone on the ground knew success, meaning everyone out, depended on getting through the1000 meters of enemy controlled turf to the river edge.

It had all ended up damn well considering. None of our guys were killed. Three of the four Huey's Gunships made it back to fight another day. One had been hit by a North Vietnamese rocket as it was offloading its SEALs. The Chief and the radioman had taken their wounds when the rocket hit. The Pilot, Copilot, Door Gunner and SEALs had garbed every weapon they could get off the chopper and joined in on breaking through to the river's edge.

During the fight to the river bank the 4 PBR's where hauling ass up river to get themselves in position. The Seawolf's kept up air-support, killing anyone they could on our guys flanks or between them and the river's edge. On the ground you had 4 Army Rangers, 3 Navy Seawolf's crew and 14 SEALs. Shorty told me later "We had them out numbered; It was only 10 of them to 1 of us!" The one wounded Ranger Medic and two SEAL Corpsmen had patched and killed as they went, patching ours and killing the bad guys. All except one bad guy they kept alive and brought out with them. After all they were there to gather Intelligence

It took about an hour and half to fight their way to the river's edge. The Seawolf's had picked a small point in the bend of the river and kept everyone moving in that direction. When they had themselves on the point and where ready to be extracted: Three of the PBR's had headed straight at the point, at 30 Knots plus. About 30 feet from running the vessels on to the bank they had reversed their water jets spun the boats around and planted the stern up against the river bank. God Bless the Brown Water Navy they could spin and stop those boats on a dime.

One PBR and three Seawolf's were now doing all the firing from our side. The three PBR's crews and our guys were busy getting everyone on the boats, wounded first. As soon as all hands where loaded, the PBR's had hit full water-jets and where speeding down river at 30 + knots: Everyone had been loaded and out of there in under 2 minutes. It had been a good day: None of ours dead, bunches of theirs meeting their maker.

When an Operation is done, it's not done even for the wounded. All four Rangers and two of our guys where shot up. They would be debriefed in the hospital as soon as medically possible. For the rest of the guys it was now: No talking about the Operation, clean yourself, your weapons and go straight into debrief. Our Officers and Chiefs did the Debriefs and forwarded them on.

Well that's the way it was usually done but not this time. As soon as the PBR's had hit the dock in Canto, the wounded, already patched up, where taken to the main military hospital in Canto. Everyone else went straight into debrief by what they later found out where CIA.

When the four Rangers LURPS had figured out they were facing at least a full company of North Vietnamese Regulars everything had changed. Their normal Operation was NO-Contact, maintain radio silence and report what you see when you get back. Being that no one had ever heard of North Vietnamese Regulars this far into South Vietnam everything was out the window. They had known the SEALs where monitoring there normally quite radio frequency.

It was a private deal they, Marine Recon and Seals operating around Canto area had. In those days Spec Ops where many times left out on the limb by themselves. We took care of each other as best we could. The Rangers had figured they where goners, as slow as the rest of the Army moved. They just wanted to make sure the word got out and got out fast!

Well it did and in spades, the Regular Army top brass where highly pissed. Too bad, by the time the PBR's hit the dock, the Spooks where in charge with a direct line to Washington D. C. Normally a thing that pissed us all off: This war was being run out of the White House. In this case a good deal as the Rangers asses were saved for going outside Army top brass.

When I flew in to join Det. "Alpha" everything was being run under the Spooks and for good reasons. The

North Vietnamese Officer that the Rangers had captured was spilling his guts under spook integration techniques. Not what you would consider your Mom & Pop questioning secessions. I don't care what some damn do gooders say: These techniques are very effective when done by an expert. It boiled down to, what Military Intelligence considered impossible "Battalion size North Vietnamese Units in the Mekong Delta".

By the time I arrived it was already well established fact that the North Vietnamese where there. Two days after my arrival both Fire Teams of Det. "Alpha" made No Contact Insertions, one Fire Team on the East side, one from the West side. There had been so many of them that the Operation was a Pucker Factor 8 for me. Everyone got in and out undetected but you felt like any second someone would sneeze and they would be on us like stink on skunk!

What made my second operation with Det. Alpha and last Op in the Nam a Pucker Factor 10: The B-52's where on their way from Okinawa, Thailand & Guam before we even Inserted. Each would be caring 108, 500 pound bombs. There would be wave after wave of them dropping their bombs in the area we had designated as part of the North Vietnamese build-up area. If we did not get out green frogmen asses out there before they started dropping we where screwed. Now it might not sound to bright, going in on a mission, just before the raid but "The Powers That Be" needed to know what was there just before the raid, that was our job. The

U.S. Army Air Calvary, in conjunction with the South Vietnamese ARVIN's, would be doing a Battalion size sweep through the area just after the raids, picking up what was left.

If the PBR's had not, waited around well past our drop-dead Rendezvous time, I believe there would have been a bunch of dead SEALs. As it was when we finally reached our pick up point we believed the PBR's to have all ready moved off down river about 7 miles. That had been our back up plan, and not much of one at that. Hit the River and swim with the current as it moved to the sea, the PBR's would be looking for us there.

Shorty had me brake radio silence just as we reached the extraction point, the bombs where already falling: Some hitting way to close. Low and behold the PBR's sailors, at great risk to themselves, where still there. They did their; charge in, spin around stop, load us and hall ass trick. God Love the Brown Water Navy, they had saved or green frogmen asses again.

The Naval Base at Canto was 15 miles upriver from where we were extracted. You could feel, smell, taste and see the exploding bombs every inch of the damn way back. A couple times, early on, those bombs came so close to us I have no idea why we and the boats survived it. One time both PBR's where lifted clear of the water after a bomb went off in the river. The Bombs were still falling as our feet hit the PBR dock in Canto. The river, dock, land, buildings everything shook with a solid rumble. That was a PUCKER Factor 10 +, no fucking question!

John Carl Roat

Getting Out

Detachment Alpha had been extended in country for a month. Shorty had been made Chief, due to his performance in combat and their new radioman had joined them in Canto. Within five days of my last Operation in the Team, I was back in Coronado California, on the Silver Strand, mustering out of the Navy. It would have been quicker then that accept for a little mechanical failure. This caused a little partying hardy on the way home that will give you some incite as to my thought process. These flights were called, the flights "back to The Real World!"

I was booked on a civilian flight, Braniff, out of Saigon for the return flight home. There were many of these type of flights used to bring home Army or Marine Troops that had done there year in country. If a combat troop got a Braniff flight he had scored big time. Not only where the planes painted in wild combinations of color but the Stewardess's where as well. Those Braniff Stewardess's loved flying the flight as well and did everything in their power make sure the troops enjoyed their long flight back to " The World"

There was a big stink about me getting on the plane and I damn near didn't make it. Everyone but me was in Uniform and could not carry weapons. I on the other hand had a Set of Orders that stated: Ware Civilian Clothing and carry Side-arm's in performance of these Duties.

The simple facts of me being in civilian clothing and being allowed to carry sidearm had focused way to much attention on me. Not a big deal in these circumstances but something I felt uncomfortable with. The Army and Marine guys had all went through three bag checks. Everything they were carrying home laid out and gone through by Military Police, MP's. I started one but never finished it!

When they had announced the first bag inspection I had presented my Orders to the Officer in charge of the MP's on the passenger line, I had one small carry on bag, In it was my Loaded Smith & Wesson 357 Highway Patrolman and a shaving kit. Of course this caused there system to have a shit fit. Team guys were allowed to use the weapon of their choice as a side arm. Most guys where carrying the new Browning 9 mm or the 1911 45. I like revolvers, fewer moving parts so less can go wrong.

My problems were mutable: 1. Under the Geneva Convention, the 357 round was not legal to kill the enemy with. The Smith & Wesson fired both the 38 Special Round and the 357 and the dumb assed MP Officer did not know the difference. Mine was loaded with 38 Special rounds, which were legal to kill the enemy with! He had started by putting me up on charges.

2. The Colonel in charge of the MP's, his title was Provost Marshal,Tan Son Nhut Airbase Saigon, did not like the fact: That a Second Class Petty Officer could

ware civilian close and carry sidearms in the performance of his duties and he couldn't.

3. My biggest problem, something hidden in my boots I was not Authorized to have in my position!

It all steamed from the Army giving some Senior Officers a free ride in the Nam. They would fly in for six months and be assigned a job with little chance of seeing any combat. It was called: Getting your Ticket Punched. Anyone who had served in a Combat Zone for 6 months got a extra points toward advancement. The Ticket Punching helped the Political non-fighting type officers keep up in the advancement competition, with the few real Combat officers the Army had. I'm not saying it is right or wrong here; just how it is! Never assume that the Military is non-political: From O-6, Marine, Army, or Air Force Colonel's and U.S. Navy Captain's, if you are not politically astute and correct; you will not advance to the upper echelons of “OFFICERDOM” Generals, Admirals and the like.

As they where escorting me away from the passenger area to the Provost Marshal's office I spotted my Marine mentor, Sergeant Brooks. He was following our little procession with his eye's. Two things struck me wright off the bat, Brooks was now a Master Sergeant E-8 and he was paying close attention without looking like he gave a shit. It always nice to have a set of friendly eyes looking on but the worse that would happen is missing my flight, no a biggie just a pain in the ass.

My biggest concern right now was them finding the fifteen $100.00 green backs hidden in my expensive, handmade civilian boots! Not something I was authorized to have in my possession. Green Backs,our currency where not authorized for use by military personnel in in the Nam. You had to use MPC, Military Payment Certificate, dollars where prized on the black market and bought more then they where worth at face value.

For five hours, from the time I presented my orders until that asshole was forced to escort me personally, to the already fully loaded plane: I had set in his office and listened to, call after call; of him trying to get my seat on the flight canceled. I didn't say anything but yes Sir or no Sir. It seemed to me he was getting madder as his little power trips failed. When two Spook types, CIA I had worked with; walked into the Colonels office with a two Star Army General, the Colonel's silly game was up!

They two Spooks first explained the finer points of the Geneva Convention to the dumb-ass Colonel: It was perfectly all right to kill the enemy with a 38 Special round, even if it was fired from a 357 revolver. The Two Star General then explained: "You personally, will escort Second Class Petty Officer Austin to his plane! If he misses his flight, you Colonel, will find yourself sent to a Real Combat Zone!" He had stalled so long that they had to hold the plane out on the flight-line of, at the time, the busiest airport on earth.

This flight started off different for me in two ways:

THE TERRORIST

First; my Second Class Petty Officer ass being escorted by a full Army Bird Colonel, to a Braniff jetliner being held out on the flight-line, just for little old me! As I got out of his chauffeur driven jeep, I politely said: "Thank you Sir! Might I suggest Sir; that you remove those two small Colonel's flags from your front fenders. The Viet Cong love targeting senior officers sir, no since in holding the bullseye for them Sir." Second: Master Sergeant Brooks was holding a seat for me up front with the Senior No-commissioned and Officers.

I had flown out on several of these type flights before: The three baggage inspections had nothing to do with anything but weapons; they confiscated nothing else. Booze, pot nothing, if it didn't blow up or kill people, you could keep it! Every flight was the same, until the wheels left the ground; no one said a damn thing. It was like setting in a room full of death mutes.

When the wheels left the ground: A great roar went up, out came the booze and the pot and the "Back to the World" flight party started. I don't care if you smoked pot or not, every other guy was lighting up a joint. You were going to get a contact high from even breathing. Never mind all the booze, everything from Jack Daniel's to the finest Champagne was being passed around, even most of the non-drinkers where sharing in.

What usually happened was a couple hours of smoking dope, drinking and lot of young guy Bull Shiting. Then everyone was asleep for the rest of the flight to Alaska;

not this trip! This flight started exactly the same as the other, things changed about an hour out. Everyone was stoned to one degree or another, including the Stewardess's, by then.

The pilot announced we would be making an unscheduled landing in Tokyo Japan due to minor mechanical problems. This flight had been scheduled straight through to Anchorage Alaska, for re-fueling then on to San Francisco.

Brooks and I both admittedly, had a little contact high going on, just from breathing the air in the cabin. But neither of us smoked a joint or even had a drink. We spent the time catching up on each other and on how different paths that led us both to this flight. Brooks being a little high on was much more open on personal things then I had every heard him.

For me this turned out to be a great thing; I got real time Intelligence I would need in my next profession, terrorist . Brooks would be getting out a year after I did, He was taking what they call an Early Out. Brooks had been recruited to join a new unit the the F.B.I. was forming to handle domestic terrorisms. I of course did not fill him in on my real plans. As far as he knew I was getting out and becoming a Commercial Diver.

Right after he testified in the Court-martial in the Subic Bay Philippines Brooks had gone Marine Corps Force Reconnaissance. For those of you not in the know; Recon Marines are bad asses and commonly known as Recon. If you are going to be Recon you had better be a Marines Marine and take on any damn thing that gets thrown at you. Including making bullshit smell like roses!

The Intelligence he had giving me: The FBI was forming a new unit, dealing with Counter Terrorism in the U.S.! If you remember those times; the Vietnam War protesters had blown a few thing up and killed a few people. Brooks was getting an early out as he had been recruited to be a member of that new unit. In my slightly stoned state: I had the thought, Damn do they know I'm coming? The new unit was being heavily recruited from the military units that had experience dealing with terrorist and insurgences. Right up Brookses alley.

Master Sergeant Brooks had most of his platoon of fourteen returning from the Nam with him. Eleven Sergeants E-5 , my level of rank and one U.S. First Class Petty Officers E-6, a Combat Corpsman. All Combat Corpsmen in the Marine Corps are sailors not marines. Bad asses, that can patch-up your men and keep shooting the bad guys, while they patch. They had spent the last seven months in the DMZ.

The Demilitarized Zone or DMZ. It was area between North Vietnam and South Vietnam, that both sides, had agreed: Not to have military bases or operations in. Yea right, it ran East to West from the South Chine Sea, to Laos and was a bout11/2 miles wide. Both of us had operated up there. Brooks and his RECON Platoon had spent the last 7 months kicking the NVA asses in the DMZ. Believe me I operated there and it was full of North Vietnam's troops. The NVA or The Vietnam People's Army.

Most NVA's supplies came down what was called the Ho Chi Min Trail. They used the DMZ as their personal staging area. The Trail ran just across the South Vietnam border in Cambodia, north to south. Now for reasons known to only god and our dumb dumb ass president, we let this go on. Number 1 American troops where not to be in Cambodia or the DVZ, another, Ya Right! The NVA used bicycles, elephants, trucks and the troops strong backs, to move the equipment of war from the north to where they wanted to kill us, in the south.

Since we where not supposed to be there; our side went small but Mean and BAD! Books and his platoon of Recon had been the Mean and Bad for seven months; in an area where they were out numbered 10 to 1! As we talked on the way to our new destination Tokyo: Brooks filled me in on the willful crippling, mutilation and disfigurement they had wrought on the North Vietnamese Army.

" Karl this is baddest bunch of Marines that ever fucking walked" Coming from Brooks, normally not subject to speaking Bull Shit or exaggeration I was impressed. "This platoon killed more NVA and destroyed more equipment, headed south, then all the damn B-52 bombing raids of the War. If this lay-over in Japan is more then a few hours I'll see that my Marines have a good time!" My comment: Master Sergeant Brooks I know Tokyo it like a book, the Paris Steam Baths is just the place!

When we landed in Tokyo the plane was found to have more than a minor problem; this was going to take a while. After about an hour they got everyone off the plane and into the civilian terminal. All E-5 and above where mustered in an area down the concourse from the rest of the troops. For the second time in one day I was in the hands of, a not very bright, Army Colonel.

This was the good part of his dumb assed plan: Each group of 8 would have an E-5 of above in charge. Hotel rooms had been arranged in the down town Tokyo area about 20 miles away. We would be transported to the hotels by cab. Now for the not very bright part: According to this Colonel "You are responsible to see that no-one leaves the hotels, gets drunk, consorts with whores or otherwise defames the United States Military!" My first thought: NO FUCKING WAY!

Now anyone, that served in the Nam, knows the Army and Marines combat troops lived in the bush like animals. They never lost any major battles and had few senior officers that they looked up to. Why you ask? Because the Enlisted did a minimum of a year in country! The senior officers in most cases where taking care of their own comfort. They were rarely in country more than 6 months and in most all cases never lived like animals in the bush!

These guys were battle hardened troops who rarely had anyone to respect above a Sergeant or Petty Officer, E-5's to E-9's. That's one damn thing I can say for Team Officers sailors all; they did what we did and lived where we lived. During the Nam war every Senior, UDT or SEAL Officer that got to the Nam: Made sure they saw combat, one damn way or another.

To make a long story short; the senior Enlisted man on the flight was Master Gunnery Sergeant Brooks. There he was up front standing by the dumb-ass Colonel, looking like a mean bad-assed Recon Marine, that would eat steel to enforce the Colonel Orders. I'm sure the Colonel believed that, I didn't. Brooks gave the Army Colonel a sharp Salute, "Sir I will handle this smartly! I will report to your office sir when I have it accomplished, may I use my E-6 Corpsman to assist me Sir?" The Colonel returned the salute and said " Permission granted, I need this underway within the hour Master Sergeant" and walked off.

Brooks did not bat an eye. Corpsman Rogers you will be coming with me and address the rest of the troops. Corporeal Bancroft you and Petty Officer Austin will take this hotel and personnel list and make group assignments. Each of the rest of you will show Corporal Rogers your ID Card, Dog tag and confirm that he has your correct name and Serial Number by Initialing the it on his roster! When he has assigned troops and given you your roster, Petty Officer Austin will, assign Hotels and see that you have transportation.

With that he handed Bancroft the personnel roster, me the hotel list and off he and his Corpsman went. I quickly scanned the hotel list. Right there was was better then what I had hoped for, a hotel less then a block from the Paris Steam Baths: We had 20 rooms booked in The New Tokyo Hotel. All I had to do was assign the Recon guys and myself those rooms and make one phone call! As it worked out the the Colonels order to Brooks " I need this underway within the hour" was not only underway but almost completed. Just Recon and myself standing by at the Airport to be picked up; my one phone call had been more successful then I had hoped for!

My call had been to a CIA guy I knew that worked out of Japan. He was the same guy, Master Chief Henily and I had pulled off the operation for in Philippines. Henily bringing me into that OP to get the Big Huk and its successful conclusion had greased my way with the Spooks. I had worked for this man several times since and he was one of the few Spooks I fully trusted.

The Paris Steam Baths was one of the finest Whore Houses anywhere and it was a front business for the CIA. It took up all a full city block and was four stories high and had: The finest women. steam baths, private parties room, restaurants and any other accommodation of male pleasure you could think off.

Of course they had area's set up for the express purpose of gathering blackmail information; these where wired for sound and film. They also had areas that were swept to make sure there were no damn recording devices. In these they debriefed men that where working for them undercover.

The Spook handled it all including the dumb assed Colonel! He had called the Colonels boss, a General and explained the the CIA wanted to Debrief Brooks and his platoon on their Ops in the DMZ. They would arrange their transportation and housing and of course, mew, Petty Officer Karl Austin had been included.

We where picked up at the airport in a fancy civilian bus with a wild paint job and heavily tinted windows. It was kind of funny and not very clandestine to my way of thinking: A bunch of camie clad Marines standing around in front of the civilian air terminal, up pulls this movie star like bus, the driver gets off holding a sign that says: Brooks & Austin!

The look on Master Sergeant Brooks and rest of those Recon Marines faces Pure-D "What The Fuck Has This Frogman Done? I had never seen Brooks with his mouth hanging open in surprise! All I had told him was: We would all go together on one bus. Nothing about who I had called or anything about the steam baths being a CIA cover organization.

When I had called the Spook I started to outline what I wanted with the Paris Steam Baths. When I got to the part about Recon Marines and the DMZ, he stopped me and said "give me a name". I said "Master Sergeant Brooks" he said "no problem done deal! Tell me this

Coronals name" I told him, "how long before your ready to be picked up" about an hour, "have everyone out front of the civilian terminal when your ready, there will be a bus!"

When we saddled up on the bus the Spook was on board. Brooks a got a big shit eating grin on his face. It was one of those; it's a small world moments. A broken down Braniff jet and my phone call had given the CIA a way to thank the men that had done such a great job for them on the Hoe Che Min Trail and the in the DMZ. This thank you, would be Warrior style: Knee wobbling, guttering crawling, women filled drunken LUST! And every damn bit of it was with: Beautiful women that could sing, dance, message and screw you brains out with stile!

We never saw the rooms at The New Tokyo Hotel. The bus took us straight into a large garage attached to the Paris Stem Baths. Off the bus and straight into the spooks forth floor debrief area. No hidden recording devices or so I had been told! With them you where only told whatever they wanted you to hear! I trusted this spook because I done five ops for him since that first one with Chief Henily in the PI. Everything with them was "need to know" and if they thought you needed to know a lie; they told you a lie! So who knows there may be movies with sound of the whole damn night!

The fourth floor had it's own restaurant, steam baths, group and private rooms. There was a Debrief, of sorts between the spook and Brooks; it lasted all of thirty minutes! Then if was fucking on; the last drunk of my life! On every level it was, let it all hang out time. No group on this earth hangs it out there higher then young warriors when the battles are done and they still live! The number one reason: You owe it to your Brothers of the Sword that didn't make through the battles! No other fucking reason counts!

It started with Stakes not just any stakes; Kobe Stakes, the finest dam meat on earth. The ladies out numbered us at least two to one. All hotter then hell, looked like the home coming queen but Pure-D high classed hooker. They were not dressed like geisha girls!

Everyone one of them were wearing Bikini's. American Rock and Roll was the background music and Jack Daniels and good old U.S. of A. beer flowed. The group attitude was: “Eat Shit and Howl at the Moon a warriors death comes all to soon! Enjoy Brothers!.” I will assure you we did!

After stakes is was; steam baths and massage,at the hands of bikini clad babes. These ladies knew what they were doing message wise and sexually. Guys would be drifting away to the private room with one, two or three of the ladies at time. The only other two “Events” I'll share with you the reader that night are: The Drinking Contest I all most won and The Dance of the Flaming Asshole, my contribution to the floor show!

The drinking contest started out with a beer guzzling

contest that I instigated. We made that one, a Navy against Marines, contest. Since there Corpsman and I where the only two sailors the marines, Brooks included, all slammed a timed pint of Guinness! I had picked the beer because I knew it properties: A heavy dark beer, brewed from roasted grains added to the coffee beans.

The game goes like this: A lull pint sitting on the bar top the player hold it with his hand. The time runs from the time you pick it up till it's on the bar top empty. The best time any of the Marines put up was 4 seconds, I thought I had this one hands down, my best is 3 seconds flat my worst timed was 3.7!

Anyway the Navy where Number one and two! Their Navy pecker checker, military slang for Corpsman, Rogers was number 1 with 2.9 seconds! I was number 2 with 3.1 seconds! Of course the Recon guys where all screaming they won because he was their platoon pecker checker. Rogers put a stop to that with " Admit two sailors kicked your ass or: The next time you need a clandestine shot for the Clap you'll have to kiss my sailor ass before you get it" No one wants the Clap, gonorrhea, in their medicals records. The Bad Ass-ed Recon Marines caved and admitted the Navy won!

Now the Dance of the Flaming Asshole is widely believed to be a bit of SEAL Team barbarity. No so, UDT members where taught this dance by Army Special Forces A Teams, well before Seal Team was even commissioned! The SF Snake Eaters had learned it from the Montagnards a group of Ingenuousness mountain people in Vietnam and Cambodia. It is one of a number of rights of passage to manhood for the Tribe. All though they did use, a gas soaked material much like a burlap sack, instead of the toilet paper we use.

I did it the way Special Forces taught us: Wrap and twist toilette paper into a wick about two and half feet long. A lose wrap burns quicker and hotter: Make damn sure it is a tight wrap, you're going to get burned, no sense in incinerating your nut sack. My dance went over all right with a bunch of drunk Marines and over big time with the hookers. The ladies where laughing their pretty little Japanese ass off. Since I was drunk and doing, not watching from a distance, I'll describe a legendary Dance of The Flaming Asshole I watched!

We did a lot of our winter training down in Saint Thomas, Virgin Islands. Way up on top of a mountain. overlooking the Saint T. was a exclusive Hotel called the Saint Thomas Club. They had the frame of a chapel, with no walls, It was used for weddings. When they had a wedding scheduled they would get a couple Team guys to cut fresh palm fronds and lash them to the chapel frame. It took one overflowing stake truck full of the damn palm fronds and one day of labor to get it done. Your pay would be: A night on the Club, nice room, great dinner and of course unlimited drinks. The Clubs mistake was in hiring the two guys they did, Jesse and Van!

This place was classy and owned by two Producers

from New York. They were both queerer then three, threes for a nine dollar bill. They produced Musicals and both could sing, dance and play the piano like no tomorrow. The clubs floor show was in a huge circular, glass walled room. So everyone was looking out over Saint Thomas twinkling lights below.

I guess you would call the ambiance; "a romantic setting". The entertainment was always high class not the usual hairy assed frogman fair! When the show was ready to start, the lights would dim, only small lite candles on each table. The owners had two Baby Grand Pianos set in front and they would do a dulling pianos thing with some classical music. Our boys Van and Jess where about to strike!

It went down like this: Several of us made a semi circle around out teammates, as soon as the lights were dimmed. they dropped their pants, stuck their pre-rolled toilette-paper wicks in their frogman assholes. They bent forward at a forty-five degree angle and the wicks where lite! With their pants down around their ankles, bent over, it gave them the perfect stomping shuffle!

They started stomping and shuffling out amongst the dimly lite tables. It took at least a couple minutes before anyone could figure out what they where seeing. A few people , thinking it was part of the show, started clapping.

Then it was gasp, a few screams and people trying to

get the hell out of their! I think you get the drift of the dance I did for that night for my Recon brothers and our ladies of the night! And yes I got my thighs and sack burned that's part of the dumb assed dance!

The flight out of Tokyo the next day was an different plane with a different destination; Hawaii, refuel and clear Customs, on to Sand Diego. The flight was long enough that my abused body and mind where in sink by the time we reached Hawaii. We would only have about 3 hours, enough time to clear customs and get something to eat and back on the plane. As Brooks and I BS-ed our way to San Diego the feeling I get, when bad shit is getting ready to test me, came on!

It starts with the a quote coming to my mind. No one seems to know who first said it, I heard from Chief Henily, who didn't know. He brought it up one evening while we sipped his good Scotch and waxed philosophically on life and death. He first said: "Never let them see you sweat! Or as the unknown poet said:" "Fate whispers to the warrior, you cannot withstand this storm! And the warrior whispers back, I am the storm!" Somehow that short simple chain of words became: My hair on the back of my neck, my feeling that I had better be ready, shit was coming.

We didn't land at the civilian airport, we landed at the Navy field on North Island, across the bay from Sand Diego. As the plane taxied up to the terminal I could see Fate whisper was getting ready to be tested. Out the window, standing on the tarmac just out side the terminal: There stood brother Jim, Judith Jo, Chief Jimmy Henily and a Navy Chaplain I knew, that worked with the Teams. I looked at Brooks and said: " Brother I'm going to get off the plane last! I can see bad news waiting on the tarmac. I need to do this alone so I'll get in touch later"

I already knew it meant death close and personal! Just from the people standing outside the terminal, it was family not warrior brothers. The military in general and the Teams particularly, have a from, a set way they handle death. Everything from notification of loved ones to putting the casket in the ground. I had done four escorts of remains, two notification of loved ones, attended six Team member services and done four presentation of colors to Team widows. Oh ya I knew the routine!

Jim and Judith Jo had been married in a large ceremony that her dad had insisted on. If the Chief was giving up his daughter it would be done in stile! As it turned out they had been married, with Boats, doing Best Man duties for us both. And me. I was in the Delta, doing by best not to be blown up by our own B-52s. As it turned out I was safer then most of my loved ones that day.

END GAME

After I got off the plane there were few subdued hand shakes and hugs. Then Chief Henily guided everyone to a small conference room In the Navy Terminal. Like my mother, I knew I would handle whatever came calmly, at least until panic or tears didn't matter. I was keying on Henily, my warrior brother, we had both done this to many times. Henily's was wound tighter then I had ever seen him so it was worse then I could imagine.

The plain truth was: My Mother, Dad one brother and sister along with Judith Jo's Dad, the Chief, her mom, both sisters and Boats where dead! They had all died at hands of one drunken teenage driver. Now you know why our wild night in Tokyo was the last drunk of my life, I have not had a drink since. I had sat their as, Judith Jo told me the story of how it had happened, with my brain screaming: I DRIVE DRUNK, over and over. I have never had another drink and never will!

After the reception Jim and Judith Jo had taken off for parts unknown in Baja California. Everyone else in both families had piled in a rented Limo for drive back to San Diego from Cardiff. In those days a rural area about 25 north of San Diego, a small hilly, farming community along the ocean. The wedding had been held on a hill over a farm land and the sea.

From the time I graduated from boot camp till the day of their death Dad and Chief had been best friends. Too look at the two of them you would never understand why: Dad looked like Mr Straight Arrow and in fact he was. It was the Chief, with the Eyeball tattooed in middle of his forehead, hula girls on his ear lobes, chains around his neck and wrist, that didn't look like what he was; a man of honor, a family man. Our two families had been like one.

The Limo was going south on 101 the coast highway and had the green light at an intersection. A drunk teenager speeding, ran the red light coming from west to east. He was driving a station wagon at about 60 miles an hour. The police had told my brother; that by itself did not have the mass to kill everyone in the limo. It did have the mass to drive the limo into the south to north lane where a fully loaded Tractor Trailer rig finished the job. Nine members of our combined families were dead. The truck diver made it ten dead, only the drunk driving teen lived.

The next few days and nights where a strange mix of: A Strangle-hold on my emotions and completely letting go. During the day going through the process of getting out of the Navy, not a simple task. In the evening spending time with Jim and Judith Jo and sharing our grief in a semi-normal way. At night by myself bawling like a baby, until I fell asleep exhausted. No one on this earth knew anything about my terrorisms plans. Not even that I had had a thought in that direction and I damn well had to keep it that way.

The Teams of course had finally found out I did not

have a Secret Clearance. This caused a whole lot of shit! Fingers were being pointed, phone calls being made, faxes back and forth and interviewers of me by: the Naval Intelligence. FBI and one Spook I didn't know.

The truth of the matter is that none of them had done their do-diligence, so the pack of them, where going to look like shit if they couldn't pin it on someone else! I of course had no idea about the destruction of my family but I did have a good idea what was coming on the: No Secret Clearance issue and I was ready.

There is a tried and true method of investigation and Interrogation, that short of drilling your teeth, will work about 95 percent of the time. The Commander from Naval Intelligence, the FBI Agent and the CIA Spook would each toke turns with me. The Commander had been mister nice guy. The The FBI Agent had a skeptical but polite attitude and the CIA Spook was all secret agent bad ass. In the end, if there where a lie-detector all three would be in on the test.

It would be held in a bare room with; the polygraph technicians, myself and the three investigating officers. When that came down they would all, but the technicians, be aggressive and doubtful of everything I said. The tech would sit their all calmly marking on the chart! They could do it one of two ways: One of them asking all the questions with the other two applying pressure by staying in my view looking like the didn't believe a thing I said. Or each asking different questions that jumped all over the place.

The reasons it wouldn't work on me were twofold:

1) I knew the techniques through and through to include, how to beat, the dread Polygraph or lie-director. The Polygraph works only if you allow it to. In other words; if you can lie and control your heart rate and respiration, the machine will say you are telling the truth when your lying out your ass. Like many of the things I would use in being the terrorist, I had learned it from the CIA.

2) I put a stop to the Polygraph test because of one question I was ask and my emotional exhaustion.

All I had to do was just stick to my story about having filled it out twice; once after graduation and again when the said they didn't have it when I shipped over! I had gone over everything they might ask me for last six months knowing this was coming: Who did you give it too? "I don't know his name but he was the black shoe Yeoman at UDT 21 had when I graduated into the Teams. The second time the same thing but a different Yeoman. At the time of me coming into and shipping over in the Teams we were short handed. Many of the support personal were only there for a couple week and no one knew who did what.

I had planed to go through the whole process including the lie-detector but at the end of my third interview I put a stop to it. Each of their interviews had had some different and some over lapping questions. During the Commander from Naval Intelligence part of the interviews; he had been mister nice guy but he had broached Fine's murder. " Wasn't their some murder investigation you were involved in?"

My answer had been: "Well sort of. Before I came to the teams some police department had requested and Interview. The X.O., of the Saratoga had told them I would be available when the ship reached Pearl Harbor Hawaii in a few days but they never showed up. If I remember right, the X. O. had me make a statement to out legal officer and sent it on to the states. "

The Commanders question had been a Red Flag for me: These guys had gone deeper then I had thought they would and I needed to put an end to this shit. You might say, due to the loss of most of my family, I was not at my emotional best and had little sleep over the last few days. I had never done a Lie-detector at this level of emotional stress and lack of sleep.

The FBI guy had covered the general areas I had expected from past experience. Mainly family history, outside interest and what did I think happened to my Secret Clarence. The Spook questions was all over the place with no particular order. The A-hole had even brought up the Paris Steam Baths and a few of the ops I had done for the CIA. As part of the interview came to an end the Spook had said: "I think you're fucking lying Austin! You're going to take a Polygraph Test!" I had these assholes by by the balls and I knew it. Time to change plans and play a little hard ball.

Only low level Spooks do these kinds of exit interviews, I knew his job better then he did. So I told him: Listen up asshole, I'll take your fucking lie-detector test! But I'm not the one that fucked up here! It's the CIA, Naval Intelligence and the fucking Teams! All three have had me involved in Top Secret operations for six damn years. Some of them, with your clearance level, your not qualified to know about! It seems to me there has been a bunch of fucking up here. Since I had no clearance and worked for several Spooks higher up the food chain then you, maybe you had better talk with them about it! Let me know when or if I'm testing!

That evening my time with Judith Jo and Jim was more like it ought to have been since I got home. Talking about our loved one and sharing memories! The two families had been cremated and and places in a crypt together.

Most people could not imagine why Dad and Chief where such fast friends. Believe me it had nothing to do with appearances and everything to do with family and a mans place in it! I found out a lot of things about the Chief that I hadn't known. One I'll share with you, the targets of my strange form of terrorisms, is the Scrub Table incident from Boot Camp.

My actions had cost my Chief more them I had known. In truth it had cost him more then it had me. I had lost my boot camp Recruit Athletic Petty Officer stripe for kicking the shit out of a Recruit Chief Petty Officer from another Boot Camp Company.

It seems that the other Companies real Chief was as mush of a prick as his Recruit Chief Petty Officer whose ass I had kicked. He had made Judith Jo's dad agree to cover his next four duty weekends or he was pushing for me to go to the brig! Since I was guilty has hell if the other companies chief had pushed for Court-martial it would have happened. Hell they even could have kicked me out of the Navy! Like my Dad the Chief had always gone the extra mile for me.

The Naval Intelligence officer, the FBI Agent and the CIA Spook folded! As I had thought they would. It was decided that I would sign a document in which I swore: I would never disclose any secret of the United States that I was privileged too. Like I said before anytime anyone mentions security to you think: Security My Ass! I'm going to conclude the; learn about about me part of this book by giving you the answer to why: I didn't kill the dumb assed young boy that had murdered our family with his car?

Brother Jim and I had the conversation on this the first night I was home. Of course away from Judith Jo presents. It seems she had broached the topic with Jim as to. what I would do, when I found out what happened! Jim who had never even thought of killing anyone and is truly a caring Mr. Nice Guy, was struggling with the thought of murder, when she asked.

Not something he had admitted to her at the time. We both came to the same conclusion, for the same reason. Jim over several days of deep anger and thought: Me, I knew immediately! Both of us had been drunken drivers, something all to many young guys do!

I'm use to killing and in most cases it doesn't bother me at all. There are two exceptions: My murder of Petty Officer First Class Gary Fine and what the military calls Collateral Damage. All Collateral Damage means is: Your dead because you where to close to what or who was to be destroyed.

It was immediately clear to me, the teenage boy, would be more at peace dead then living with the ghost of my family in his head. Jim had come to the same conclusion after of struggling with himself and hate for several days. What had brought finally him to that point was watching the young man at his arraignment on charges for Vehicular Manslaughter and Drunken Driving. In short; the asshole would have to live with it!

Most of what I've told you to this point, you will be able with little work, to fact check. Some of the operational things I'm sure in the end our government will attempt to prosecute me for disclosing. Such as my first kills in the PI. Myself, both governments and everyone involved are prosecutable under international law! Not something that should have ever seen the light of day.

Here is what you need to know. Brooks and his FBI

Counter Domestic Terrorism Unit were finally close to figuring out it was me. Or at least the me I was, just before I had them presented with the evidence. When I had figured they were getting close, I had made a per-planned move.

I sent my Sea Daddy, Senior Chief Jimmy Henily, a package. It contained a well established false identification, the location of one million dollars in stashed cash and my apology to Jimmy. It also contained signed confessions for my first three murders, prior to joining the navy. Jimmy's Letter:

Jimmy

By the time you've received this package I'll have gone to ground, deep cover. Sorry Senior Chief but you started me on the trail I'm on. Your remember that night in the PI when you told me: "Get your head out of your ass Austin, study some fucking history! Just maybe you'll understand why, what you just said is a load of shit!". I did and came to the conclusion that our nation was about to lose what we have.

Short and sweet : I'm THE TERRORIST, the American people are giving away every freedom that all those that came before struggled to get. An overreaching federal government and a bunch of lazy me me me citizens are destroying the United States of America. Hopefully what I am doing will push them back toward living to our Constitution.

There is no conspiracy, it all me, no-one else involved, no group, just me. I know you, my family and the rest of our Green Brothers will not only be pissed off but come under close scrutiny from our oh so corrupt government. Well here is the best I can do to take a little of the sting out of that.

Brooks and his Counter Domestic Terrorism Unit have still not figured it out. They're close but not there yet. I figure they're about two to three months away.

You have two choses:

1) You can take the million and the well established false ID in the package and go to ground.

2) You can give me and everything I've sent to you, to Brooks and his team. I would bet my life, if I had to, you'll be take number 2 .

You giving me and the million up, might help convince Brooks and his bosses that no one else is involved. If you chose number 2, first contact this law firm S.F. McKnight and Associates. That firm practices constitutional law and represents me. They have been paid in advance, to find top flight representation, for those close to me that come under suspicion.

I don't want our government having a freehand with my loved ones. We both know how easy the government finds it to step outside the law. If you chose, my lawyer, Sudall Faith McKnight will attend your first meeting with Brooks. She also has a sealed packet of documents to give to the government from me.

PS: Tell Brooks that if he wants to keep his job: Sweep the penthouse apartment that The Under Secretary for Domestic Terrorism keeps at 733 15th St, Washington DC. I've had the place bugged for years. My lawyer will provide a tape she has but has not heard. That recording will prove I have not been getting my inside information from Brooks or anyone in his Unit.

PPS: I know you Shorty and the rest of my Green Brothers will never again call me Brother. That is as it should be but here is my challenge to you all: The government has one year of not terrorist activity from me, so catch me if you can!

Your Friend and THE TERRORIST

Karl Austin

Now here is why our government agreed to the publication of the book. My law firm had another package of documents they had been instructed to give to Brooks. More evidence of crimes, committed by our government. The government were assured that there would be nothing reaching the level of those documents in this book.

I did not expect them to stop their pursuit. I would not committee another act of terrorism for a year, after publication and I did tell them what my demand was to turn myself in. You will get that at end of this book. In other words, they where Blackmailed. Yes your right I'm blackmailing you as well. I want you believing that if you don't do what I ask it will get much worse!

I had begun preparing for my role as the terrorist more then six years prior to me being discharged. Most of my schooling, on how to set myself up, had come from the Spooks. Things like: Intelligence gathering, contingency planing, how to establish deep cover identification, through away one time use identification, forgery, establishing untraceable offshore banking accounts and much more. Hopefully you are smart enough to have figured out my kill skills come from my nature and my skills acquired fighting for our nations freedom!

On my discharge date I had every form of identification I would need: My own, the real me, twenty one-time only throw away forgeries and several well maintained deep cover identifications. I had, in various bank accounts and cash stashes, in excess of five million dollars. I had a thousand pounds of C-4 explosive and every weapon I might need stashed in several locations in and outside the good old US of A and I still wasn't ready. It took four more years to complete setting myself up, before I was ready for my first act of Terror. Not just for the LA attack but for everything that came after and will continue to come after I'm tried for all the crimes I have committed.

Three days after I completed my discharge fro the worlds largest nuclear canoe club, I was in Wilmington California attending Commercial Dive School. I took the six month night course. This give me time during the day to work on long range planning. The LA shut down was ready to go, as a stand alone operation by the time I completed Commercial Dive school. Why commercial diving, big pay, seasonal work, world wide and you didn't have to work for one employer. In other words you wouldn't be missed if you weren't there!

All those years ago when I had learned to sew, I had started banking every penny of my Military pay. So that was clean money with a path could be traced. I took one hundred thousand of that and invested in a start up welding & fabrication company with two Special Forces guys I knew from the Nam. That company now is the largest in the western united states. All legal as silent partner, I would just get my share of profit and they would supply me a secure storage and hook-up on site at the facility for my motor-home.

Over the next four years I did the same type of deal in seven major cities around the country. All different types of business, like the small trucking business in Boston. That start up was with Ronald Bertram Flacktum A.K.A. Shorty.

Five of the seven business arrangements turned into extremely profitable enterprises. Between those and working as a Commercial Diver all these years I have enough honest money to be considered a wealthy man. I am sure Shorty and all my business partners would love to strangle me right now. In the end, the law firm of SF McKnight and Associates, will see they're cleared of any participation or afore knowledge. Just like my family and Henily and Brooks they are a clean as fresh snow.

My honestly earned seed money, at the time of my discharge, had been just over seven hundred thousand dollars, my earnings plus interest. Where did the remainder of the four plus million come form? Straight out an R & R trip I had taken to Bangkok Thailand. In those days Thailand was a major hub for Drugs, and child molesters, pedophiles, which I had no idea of until I got there. The trip out of the combat zone in the Nam had in fact not been rest and recuperation. The who, that showed me what was going on in Bangkok and all over Thailand is of no concern. Suffice it to say that many child molesters died during that short trip and I came back to Nam one pissed off sailor. It also gave me the my source for ill gotten funds the drug trade: all that money came from carefully planed operations against the financiers of the drug trade.

The part of the Los Angles California shut down that the public saw was the most spectacular traffic jam in history. It had in fact shut down about 80% of commercial activity in LA for the day and made the front pages around the world. Where I had gone wrong was assuming that the press would make sure the whole story was told.

What you were never told by the press is: The Edmonston Pumping Plant that pumps water over the Tehachapi Mountains into Los Angles, the Los Angeles Aqueduct pipeline in Antelope Valley and Hinds Pumping Plant brings in water from the Colorado river, all had been set to blow with C-4 explosive. My mistake was in not setting the charges off.

I had thought setting real charges with the firing caps not installed but wrapped in a note at each location would be sufficient. What I had not anticipated is the press not informing the public. For years they had been anti-government and would publish anything that made the United States look ineffective. My mistake was not understanding that the press didn't hate our government, they hated out Constitution. Each note started with “You want to put me out of the Terrorist business? Start to live to our Constitution again!”

The traffic jam had been caused by cars, dropping tire spikes, as they drove through the four main clover leaf interchanges of the Los Angles freeway system at 7:00 in the morning. The trunks of each car had been modified to allow the six pointed, inch and a quarter long spikes to be dropped in a controlled manner. At the same time the traffic jam was going on the four major new out lets in Southern California received the following note with the location of the explosive charges

"THE TERRORIST

You must: Start to live to our Constitution again! This traffic jam is nothing compared to what I could have done. You will find the charges I set by following these directions. Edmonston Pumping Plant; Bottom of the of pumping basin, the Aqueduct Pipeline in Antelope Valley: Charge at mile 18 point, the Hinds Pumping Plant: Charges under all three pipes at the first bend above the pumps."

For anyone not living in the LA area: If those charges had been set off not only Los Angles but most of Southern California would have lost over 80% of all water supply immediately. In short they have to bring most of their water in from Northern California and the Colorado River. These pipelines are in access of one hundred twenty inch diameter.

Oh they looked and found the charges but didn't communicate a word to the public. Not being able to communicate my warnings and demands to the public was a serious problem that I had to carefully think out. It was also a serious flaw in my years of careful planning. I purposely secured all my operations for a year to review all planning for other flaws.

This is the highest Government Official in charge of all counter terrorisms operations in the United Stated: Under Secretary for Domestic Terrorism, Hillman R. Collific. I know everything he does. I direct the following demands to him:

1) Make public your full list of my Terrorist acts: You withheld the knowledge from the public get it done! (As a tease to the public here are a few)

(a) Black out of New York City in 1977

(b) Unplanned Emergency Shut Down Tennessee Valley Authority nuclear plants.

(c) Smith Mountain Dam Failure

(d) Rupture of Thirty-six inch Oil and Gas Trunk line Gulf of Mexico

(e) Simultaneous overpass failures on: I-10, I-90, I- 40 and I-25

2) A majority of State Attorney Generals, minimum number twenty-six, sue the Federal Government over UN-constitutional use of power. The law-firm of S.F. McKnight and Associates will supply a short list of possible suits. <u>You must go forward with one!</u>

3) Fulfill the above two demands and agree with my lawyer as to the order of trial, for the crimes I will be charged with. I will turn myself in and plead guilty to the first three murders outlined in this book.

Now the government can waste it's year of grace on a capture or kill program no problem, it will fail. So it is up to the people to get off your lazy me me me asses and force our government to agree. It's this simple I do not have to make another move to do anything, except stop what is already set to happen. Re-read (e): Brooks and his team know I am an expert in explosives and timed delay. There are more then one TERRORIST actions set and ready to go! One only five days after the time is up. You won't find them or even know how many there are.

You Choose: Live to the Constitution or live with me, THE TERRORIST!

JOHN CARL ROAT

Author of: Class 29 The Making of U.S. Navy SEALs, Graduate BUDS Class 29 , 1963 Little Creek VA. A member of: U.S. Navy Underwater Demolition Teams 21, UDT 11 and SEAL Team 1.

Since 1969 I have worked as a Commercial Diver and Dive Supervisor for: Surface Air, Surface Gas and Saturation Diving. I am a Member of the Board of Directors Divers Association

Currently working on the second book in the trilogy THE TERRORIST Crimes.

Made in the USA
San Bernardino, CA
07 April 2016